D1478259

La Llorona
Encounters with the Weeping Woman

La Llorona

Encounters with the Weeping Woman

Judith Shaw Beatty

emtippettsbookdesigns.com

What They're Saying About
La Llorona
Encounters with the Weeping Woman

"An excellent, easy-to-read addition to any Southwest book collection and a great way for newcomers to the area to acquaint themselves with local lore."

--Las Vegas, N.M. Optic

"Leaving the stories in the voice of the speaker is one of the book's most successful traits...Some nice descriptions of an older Santa Fe are included... The stories are fun."

--The New Mexican, Santa Fe

Foreword

When asked to illustrate a book about *La Llorona* by someone named Beatty I said to myself, "Sigh. Another Anglo writer appropriating New Mexican culture." I expected another example of how people get it all wrong – like the "kiva fireplace." That is an irritatingly misleading term for a fireplace style that has nothing to do with kivas but has become the standard term in real estate, architectural literature, even fiction. Meanwhile, the real story of our unique adobe fireplace is lost to history. So I was predisposed to hate it before I even read this book.

When I had finished gobbling every last word with delight and fascination, I just wanted to know how someone named Beatty managed to get this material. I recognized these voices as those of my grandparents, their peers and neighbors, and the tone of the stories mirrored a trust and intimacy that would never have been extended to the usual writer from Mainstream America looking for a good story.

Turns out Judith married into the culture, found an entrée into the vibrational field we call "la plebe," and was automatically immersed in the world from which these stories come. (When you marry a Hispanic you also marry "plebe" – the whole extended family and a community – always for better *and* worse.) That explains why these stories have the ring, the accent, the body language, code words and signals of authentic rural oral tradition. So where is the line between appropriation and appreciation?

Beatty just doesn't go there. Except for light-handed editing with an ear for colloquial dialect, she has not written a book about *La Llorona* – she made a space for the storytellers to speak in their own voices.

Besides – *La Llorona* is universal. Patriarchy is global and women weep along the waterways of all countries. But second to Chinese, more women weep in Spanish than any other language. The archetype of *La Llorona* is particularly central to the Hispanic psyche. So when I was asked to illustrate this book, deep chords began to vibrate in my native-born New Mexican memory.

It was like channeling – like conjuring her up in all her colloquial aspects, different accents and inviting her to tell her BIG story, the message The Weeping Woman is crying out in all the languages of the world. She said she weeps for equality, for justice, for patriarchy to recognize the rights of women to our own bodies.

Anita Otilia Rodriguez
April 1, 2019
Ranchos de Taos, New Mexico

Introduction

La Llorona, "the weeping woman," is as well known to the descendants of the Spaniards in the Hispanic world as the bogeyman is to some Anglo cultures, and there are probably as many different stories of this legendary phantom woman as there are people who tell them. As customs and traditions vary from village to village or from one region to the next, so do the versions of *La Llorona* and her plight as she searches in vain for her lost children. While *La Llorona* can be found in Celtic and North African cultures (as well as in the Bible), certainly the most haunting, memorable, and terrifying tales of all seem to come from the American Southwest.

Before Hernando Cortés arrived with his *conquistadores,* the Aztec Indians nightly heard the ghostly screams of Cihuacóatl, a pre-Colombian earth goddess ruling childbirth and death, whose cries of, "My children, we must flee," echoed throughout the stone canyons of Tenochtitlan. Ten years later, her dire warnings came to fruition with the arrival of Cortés. Aiding him in his conquest of the New World was *La Malinche* – "The Tongue" – his beautiful Indian interpreter and mistress whose role of translator facilitated the downfall of her own people. Years later, when Cortés announced to his mistress that he would return to Spain without her but with their young son, *La Malinche* pierced her heart and that of the child with an obsidian knife. Today, it is believed by many that *La Llorona* and *La Malinche* were one and the same person.

When the northern outpost of the Spanish Empire in America was colonized, the Spanish settlers brought *La Llorona* with them. The tales shared around the campfires during the long trek north from Mexico City can still be heard today from the *visabuelos* – great grandparents – still living in the remote villages of the Southwest, and the stories continue through the generations in rich variety.

Of all the variations heard today, the most popular one conjures up an image of the modern *La Llorona* in a black or white cloak, sometimes on horseback and sometimes on foot, wandering the arroyos, *acequias* and riverbeds, weeping and wailing for her lost children. Whether these children have been lost, accidentally drowned, or murdered outright by their infamous mother depends upon the storyteller.

Whether *La Llorona* is nine feet tall and floating across a creek, a ball of fire rolling in someone's direction, or a gnomish little person with warts on her nose, she almost always manages to terrorize her wayward victims into some sort of religious conversion or, failing that, into simply changing their ways.

For those who might ask which of the stories that follow is the "real" one, the answer *La Llorona* might offer is this: Whatever your reality is, that is what I am; it is for you, the reader, to decide. As is said in her own tongue, *"Cada cabeza es un mundo* – Each head is its own world."

Judith Shaw Beatty

Author Statement

I first heard about the legendary *La Llorona* in the late 1970s, when I was married to Eduardo Garcia Kraul. As a relative newcomer to New Mexico (I moved there in 1973), I was fascinated when I heard the classic story that everyone seems to know, and then was immediately hooked when I was told that there were easily a hundred other versions of the tale. The next year was spent interviewing anyone and everyone willing to share their particular story, and the result, which we published ourselves in 1988, was a book with forty-seven different accounts carefully selected from a surprisingly large collection. The updated version that you are looking at now contains fifty-six first-person accounts – I've removed some of the original ones and added a dozen more that people submitted after the first book was published.

I want to emphasize that, as someone who is not of Hispanic heritage, I have no wish to appropriate the culture or lay claim to it in any way. As a resident of northern New Mexico for forty-six years, now, I dearly love everything about it, and it is solely my goal to share these stories for everyone's entertainment as well as for posterity. Many of the contributors in the original book have since passed away, so this is their legacy.

Very special thanks is owed to Eduardo Garcia Kraul, who at this writing is 89 years old, and who brought the stories to life when the book was first published in 1988. Through him, I grew to love Hispanic culture and thus do my best to faithfully recount each story in the voice of the person who shared it. Respect.

Los Dientes

On a warm spring evening in 1945 – this was after the war was over – my father, Augustine Grace, and his brother Paul were walking down Romero Street in Santa Fe near the railroad tracks where it meets Manhattan. It was about eleven o'clock p.m. and they were returning home from the pool hall at the Recreation Club. The Recreation Club was on the Plaza and there was a motel upstairs for the tourists.

They had just passed the last house and were almost ready to cross the tracks when my father saw something bright out of the corner of his eye. He turned and saw a ball of fire rolling in their direction. He shouted with surprise and when Uncle Paul looked to see what was happening, the ball of fire turned into a bundle wrapped in a patchwork quilt. It stopped dead twenty feet from them and then just sat there. Suddenly, they heard the sound of a child crying from the bundle. They ran over to it and opened it up and there was this baby about six months old with a terrible gruesome face and big fangs. It opened its mouth as if to cry, but instead it smiled at them and said, *"Mira, Daddy, tengo dientes* – look, Daddy, I have teeth." They ran toward

West Manhattan, where my dad lived.

When I heard the story, I accused my dad of being drunk. But he wasn't. In fact, he was a man who never lied to anyone. My Uncle Paul developed a white patch on his hair after the experience. Later, all of his hair turned snow white. To this day, they swear it was the child of *La Llorona*. For many years after that, I had recurring dreams about it. In fact, they were nightmares – I'd wake up in a cold sweat.

In those days, there was a place called the Home Bakery on the corner of Romero and Agua Fria. Whenever there was some extra change, my dad would talk about getting some cream puffs or doughnuts, and I knew they would send me to pick them up. I would have to pass by that spot where *La Llorona's* baby had been seen in order to get to the bakery. There were eight of us, and I was the eldest of the boys and I was supposed to be the bravest. The fact is, I would come up with any excuse I could think of to avoid having to go there. And when I couldn't get out of it, I'd run as fast as I could to get by the spot. Nothing ever happened to me, but it was many years before the bad dreams finally stopped.

Julian Grace
Santa Fe, NM

La Llorona

The Lady Gambler

Emilio Vigil, a gambler from Las Vegas, Nevada, told this story to me:

"Before the big casinos were built and developed for the gamblers in Las Vegas, the old timers used to gamble in old shacks. The laborers that used to work in this area would spend their time playing blackjack, poker—things like that. At the time this happened it was in the 1940s. This man, a Mr. Gutierrez, and four or five other men were playing cards in one of these old shacks, and some lady came in, very young, very pretty, and she sat down and started gambling with them. It wasn't often that these men ever got to see a young beautiful woman, and this one wasn't like the so-called ladies of the street. She seemed quiet and refined and just expressed a simple and humble interest in joining them at cards. She said something to the effect that gambling was a weakness of hers and she didn't indulge very often.

"She was good, let me tell you. She played the cards like a real professional, and she was flirting with the men at the same time. Well, she cleaned a lot of them out! She sort of left them naked, if you know what I mean. Some men would come in, sit down, and twenty minutes later they would lose their

4

money to her and have to leave.

"After a while, this lady started to tap her foot on Mr. Gutierrez's shoe. She did it just a little, so he wasn't sure if she was doing it on purpose to flirt with him or if it was an accident because she was sitting so close to him at this small table. Being a vain man, however, Mr. Gutierrez figured that she was probably interested in seeing him after the game and was trying to get his attention. So he lifted up the tablecloth to look down at her foot, which was hidden by her long black skirt. At first, he thought that he was seeing things, but then he realized it was not a shoe, but a hoof. Like a deer. It took him a minute to realize that this had to be the *La Llorona* that everyone had been talking about. She had been seen all around the shacks and some said she had a cloven hoof."

Anyway, Mr. Gutierrez told me that he finished playing his hand in the game very quickly. He had already won a lot of money, but he didn't want to stay another minute!

Victor Cortez
Santa Fe, NM

El Angel De La Muerte

I have lived in Santa Fe all my life, except for when I was a baby and lived in Ranchos de Taos about a half mile from the San Francisco de Asis Mission Church, which was built by the Franciscan Fathers in the late 1700s. The church is in a plaza with fortified walls that were to protect people from the Comanche Indians, who did raids all around New Mexico for many years and did an attack on Taos in 1760. Inside the church, there is a painting of our Lord Jesus Christ. When they turn out the lights, a cross appears on the painting over Jesus's shoulder. Experts have studied this phenomenon, but no one can explain it.

My family settled in Taos in the 1500s. We are descendants of Josefa Jaramillo, who married Kit Carson. In fact, at the Kit Carson Museum in Taos, you can see a picture of her and she looks just like my mom, even down to the white streak in her hair.

In the older days, it was Spanish tradition for women to inherit and own land; in fact, women had most of the wealth. The story that has been passed down through my family is that when Kit Carson married Josefa, who was only fourteen and the daughter of wealthy Mexican parents, her inheritance fell under his control in accordance with the tradition of the *gringos*. There are many places in northern New Mexico named after Kit Carson, and he has a reputation for being a mountain man among the *gringos*. If you talk to others, especially the Navajo people, you will hear the true story of his villainous ways when he forced thousands of Navajos to walk 300 miles to Fort Sumner from Canyon de Chelly during the Civil War, and destroyed their herds and their crops and everything they owned.

When I was small, my grandmother and my mother used to say that *La Llorona* was a woman without a husband and liked to party all the time and leave her two children alone at home. She had married very young and her husband had left her with these two kids, and she began to resent them because they restricted her freedom. She would look at herself in the mirror and check for lines around her eyes and mouth and say to herself, "I've got to get my hands on another man soon before I lose my good looks." She was real vain and selfish and would spend hours applying makeup and fixing her hair.

One night, this woman got drunk and decided her kids were too much of a problem for her. She couldn't find anybody to care for them, so she just took them for a walk along the river and left them there. Nowadays I guess you would call her a psychopath. Anyway, not long after that, she got real sick with some mysterious illness and finally realized she was going to die. So while she was lying in bed waiting to die, *El Angel de la Muerte*—the Angel of Death—came down and said to her, "You can't die until you find your children." So sick as she was, she got out of bed and left the house, never to return. And her soul has not rested and it will never rest until she finds her children, and since they drowned, she is always walking along the *arroyos* and rivers looking for them.

Rose Martinez
Santa Fe, NM

She Laments But No One Listens

Children dear, come sit by my side,
so about La Llorona you may hear.
Also, how she lost her pride
and went all over seeking her lost child
without a lover.
This story is mild, for La Llorona's life
was much more wild.
For a woman her size, she put many to trial.

Many centuries ago in Old Spain, a young mother lost her only child. How she came to bring forth her child and how she lost that child is a matter of speculation, for there are as many versions as there are storytellers. As time passes, variations are added to the stories.

The story I am about to divulge is about the *Llorona* who appeared in the Mora Valley of New Mexico.

If you are acquainted with the Santa Gertrudes Valley, also known as

La Llorona

Mora, you know that the Mora River runs through the village and that this river has come to be known as *La Llorona's* highway. But this doesn't mean that she doesn't travel along or know any other routes.

Mora is a peaceful valley—most of the time. Sometimes, as you sit on your porch some quiet evening, you will hear a moaning sound. The nonbelievers will swear it is the wind brushing against the trees, but that is because they have never seen or met *La Llorona.* To the believers, it is a reality, for they have seen her and they will swear that what they hear is *La Llorona* making her way through the willows or wading in the river, for there are ripples formed there without any other logical explanation.

Many Mora residents will attest to stories about *La Llorona.* This is her home, for she always returns after a brief absence.

There are many cases where people have lost their farm animals or pets, and they will swear that *La Llorona* took them. An instance that comes to mind is the case of a poor farmer in Cleveland, one of the next villages, who lost some sheep and goats. It was reported that *La Llorona* was seen dressed in a sheepskin and crying out loud as she entered the barn where the animals had been locked up for the night. The people who saw this did nothing because they knew it was *La Llorona* and no one was willing to mess with her. Then, she suddenly disappeared. The following day, two sheep and a goat were missing and there were no signs left behind, such as tracks, so they could investigate.

Lately, very little is said about *La Llorona,* because most people want her dead. But the fact is, she is still very much alive and very real. She hasn't given up her search for her child, but I believe that now she laments the changes and contradictions that present-day life has brought about. For example, people used to go to bed early and get up early. Now, even the owls are put to shame, for people are up at all hours of the day and night. People eat food when they are driving their cars instead of at the dinner table. And where one used to visit friends in the neighboring villages, now there is no time to visit because everyone is in a hurry but with no place to go. When one needed to mind Mother Nature's call, one ran outside to the outhouse. Now, one runs into the house. And where water was once carried into the house for the residents, now it is carried outside for the animals. With all of these changes, it is no wonder that *La Llorona* laments alone!

Probably the worst change of all is that now parents are afraid of their own children, and the children are afraid of no one because *La Llorona* doesn't scare them anymore. *Que vida!* Yes, *La Llorona* still moans and howls, and people can hear her, but alas—no one pays attention to her.

Manuel B. Alcon
Mora, NM

La Llorona and the Experiments

I grew up on the Trinchera Ranch in Costilla County, Colorado. This was a working ranch consisting of tens of thousands of acres owned by the Simms family. My dad was general manager there for twenty years. It was a total paradise where we kids, all the children of ranch hands, could roam and play to our heart's content.

One night, when I was about twelve, a group of us were sitting in a circle around the fireplace at the Pacheco's house. The only adults there were Ruben and Willie, who were ranch hands, and the conversation turned to scary stories about spirits, including the super spooky *La Llorona*. You know the way it is with kids – the scarier the story, the better, so we were all ears when Ruben and Willie both lowered their voices to just above a whisper and told us that the best place to see her was down at the big sheep barn, which was south of the ranch headquarters. This was the first we'd heard that *La Llorona* was actually haunting the Trinchera Ranch, but it wasn't that much of a surprise because there were stories all over southern Colorado about various sightings of her. You could say we were a little jaded at that point, and some of us were pretty skeptical, but our curiosity overcame all of that and we begged Ruben and Willie to take us there. Willie said he couldn't go now because he had some evening chores to do. It was summer and pretty late, because it was dark outside when Ruben agreed to take us down to the barn.

So out the door our group went – there were about ten of us plus Ruben – into the night and down the trail to the sheep barn, with Ruben and his flashlight in the lead. The barn was a huge building, and there were no lights on inside. We stumbled around in the dark behind Ruben as he pulled open the loud, creaky wooden door and took us inside. It was dead quiet in there except for the rustling of the sheep moving around in the straw. Ruben lit a lantern, which cast a yellow, dim glow over all of us, and our shadows loomed like huge specters against the wall behind us.

Ruben instructed us to get on our knees and form a circle. Once we managed to do that, he stepped into the middle and said, "Okay, you kids need to repeat this prayer after me. We will pray for the spirits to bring *La Llorona* into the building." Being that we were all churchgoers, we knew how to pray and we were very respectful, and so we closed our eyes and repeated the prayer over and over, which was in Spanish. It was just a short sentence like, "Oh, spirits of the arroyos and rivers, please bring *La Llorona* to us." We really put our hearts and souls into this prayer because Ruben warned us that we had to be very sincere or it wouldn't work.

After a couple of minutes, we heard chains being banged against the building from outside. One of the kids, Michael, who was only seven or eight, yelled really loud, "IT'S THE EXPERIMENTS!!" Ruben said, "Quiet, you guys, or you'll make *La Llorona* mad!" Pretty soon, at the other end of the darkened barn, we heard the creaking of the door we had come through earlier and a loud banging of metal against metal, and then a horrible wailing and crying. One of us had to grab Michael and another kid as they tried to bolt. Ruben said, "Quiet! I think that's *La Llorona*." As we peered through the very dim light towards the door, all ten of us screamed like fools when we saw what appeared to be a woman in a white cloak with a hood enter the barn, weeping louder and louder, followed by terrible piercing screams.

Ruben said, "Stay put. You kids need to pray harder." At that point, no one was listening to Ruben. We were scared out of our minds, which was made much, much worse with little Michael's shouting at the top of his lungs, *"La Llorona,* it's the EXPERIMENTS!" None of us had any idea what the "experiments" were, but it didn't matter anymore, because we were all going to die anyway.

The moment Michael said that, *La Llorona* lunged at our little group. We were all still on our knees in that circle and some of us tried to scramble away, but it was too late. Fortunately, one very brave kid grabbed *La Llorona's* feet. Even in the dim light, we all recognized Willie's cowboy boots with their distinctive tooled leather design up the side. As Willie threw off the sheet and he and Ruben rolled around on the floor laughing, the rest of us stood around, still shaking.

Of all the experiences I had growing up on the Trinchera Ranch, this is on my top ten list as the most unforgettable.

Gerry Greeman
Indio, CA

The Hitchhiker

During the winter of 1953, I stopped at Joe's Ringside in Las Vegas, New Mexico to watch the strip show and have a few beers. It was cold, and I was tired of driving. I was on my way home to La Joya from Denver. My dad, Antonio Lucero, had a small place in La Joya about two or three miles from the Pecos River near the Greer Garson ranch. I had decided to spend the Christmas holidays there with Dad and my two brothers.

Around eleven or eleven-thirty p.m., I left Joe's Ringside and continued to La Joya. As I was driving down the hill towards Tecolote, the bright lights from my Ford illuminated the figure of a woman on the side of the road. Now, in those days, the road was a single lane, one way, and not the big freeway that is there now. I thought to myself, "What is this nun doing on the highway in the middle of the night?" Her dress was a habit of the Catholic nuns I was familiar with. I pulled the car over to a stop and reached over to open the door on the passenger side. I told her where I was headed and asked her if she wanted a ride, and she got in the car without saying a word. I could see now that it wasn't a habit she was wearing, but a dark cloak with a hood that covered most of her face. I really couldn't even see if she was young or old, or what. We passed through Bernal, San Juan, San Jose, all without her opening her mouth. I didn't mind; I was tired and didn't much feel like talking myself. Still, I tried to be polite a couple of times and ask her some questions, but she never answered me. She sat completely still, like a mannequin in a store window, with one hand on her knee and the other hidden under her cloak.

When we got to the Pecos cutoff, I was starting to get uncomfortable. Frankly, there was something about her I didn't feel right about. I began to imagine that maybe she had a knife, or maybe she was going to rob me. I had a big wad of bills in my pocket and I thought to myself, "What if she saw the money at the bar? Maybe she was in there."

As if that wasn't enough, I began to imagine the smell of sulfur, like after you've lit a match, but much stronger. That was enough for me. I stopped the car in front of Adelo's store and turned to tell her to get out of the car, but she had disappeared into thin air. Without opening the door. Then I heard this blood-curdling yell, very high pitched—terrible. It raised the hair on my neck; that's the truth. Even the dogs ran off.

I told this story to some guys at the Sunshine Bar and a guy—I don't remember his name, Freddie something—said the exact same thing had happened to some other sucker a couple of weeks before. Then he said to me, "That was *La Llorona, mula!*"

Ray Lucero
Pecos, NM

The Dentist

"Miss Martinez is ready for you, Doctor. She's a new patient and she's concerned about some dark spots on her teeth."

"Oh, great," Dr. Pace chuckled gleefully, "I need some money for my vacation coming up." It's not how you make it but how much you make, he liked to tell his colleagues. He followed Joyce, his assistant, to the operatory, where Miss Martinez lay in wait in the dentist chair.

"Is there anything that can be done about these horrible spots?" asked Miss Martinez. Her enchanting perfume and warm brown eyes set in a small pretty face almost distracted Dr. Pace from his goal.

She lay in the chair … so trusting … so vulnerable … so easy, he thought. He grunted and tsked-tsked a couple of times during the exam.

"I'm sorry, Miss, but all your teeth have to come out."

She gasped. "Isn't there something else you can do?"

"No. And it needs to be done right away or you'll destroy all your jaw bone."

Her face twisted into a mix of horror and pitifulness. "I beg you," her voice trailed off.

"Make up your mind, Miss Martinez. I'm very busy." He noticed her hesitation. "Go see someone else if you want, but the facts won't change. It has to be done as soon as possible."

She wept. He took that to mean yes. "Get the extraction setup, Joyce."

Joyce left the operatory, signaling to Dr. Pace to follow. When they reached the sterilization area she spun. "You're disgusting! Those teeth don't need to come out, you're just doing it for the money."

"Hey, eventually everyone's teeth fall out. I'm just saving her that hassle."

"I've looked the other way too long. I'm tired of your filth rubbing off on me, keeping me awake at night."

"Just quit then, I don't need you."

"That's what I'm going to do. But first I'm going into that operatory and telling that young woman you're a crook and to run, then I'm going to the dental board."

"You'll do no such thing," he snarled. "You'll get worse if you say anything to that girl. I can make sure your work reputation is ruined if you make trouble." Joyce grabbed her purse and left, slamming the door.

"Who needs that bitch," he mumbled, then returned to the operatory and extracted the young woman's teeth. She left, clutching blood-soaked gauze against her gums to slow the bleeding, weeping the whole time.

Dr. Pace eventually made a quick and cheap set of teeth for Miss Martinez, then forgot about her.

A few months later, on a stark winter evening, Doctor Pace made the daily deposit at his bank and then drove his Jaguar home. When he reached the driveway he saw someone on his front porch, waiting just out of the light. A biting wind cut through his coat as he approached his large front door.

He shivered and tightly grasped a small can of mace in his overcoat pocket. Cautiously stepping into the small cone of light on the porch, he peered into the shadow. "What do you want?"

A woman in a black hooded cloak stepped out, her face obscured. "Just to thank you."

At first he didn't recognize her, then he stepped back and tightened his grip on the mace can when he realized she was the young woman he'd pulled the teeth on a few months earlier.

"Thank you for all you've done for me. I really like my new teeth." She smiled broadly. Pretty white teeth reflected the dim light. He studied them closely. They were much better than the ones he made for her, yet they looked vaguely familiar. "Where'd you get them?"

"Why from you, silly, don't you remember?" She brushed past him as if she were floating. The icy cold air again pricked his cheek. When she reached the end of the walkway he heard a deep delicious laugh, then she disappeared into the dark.

The sound of that laugh unnerved him, causing him to spray mace in his pocket.

He fumbled again with his keys trying to get away from the choking mist. As he opened the door he became aware of something dripping off his chin. A bright red droplet splattered on the snow-white entry tile, then another, and another, quickly turning into a rain of blood.

He ran to the bathroom holding his mouth, trying to stem the flow, but the blood gushed through his fingers.

"Oh god no!" he screamed when he reached the bathroom mirror. Ragged holes in his gums marked the places where his teeth used to be. He couldn't stop the bleeding no matter how hard he pressed on the gum sockets.

The police found him the next day with dental forceps in his hand and all thirty-two of his teeth above his head in a semi-circle, spelling out a single word: L L O R O N A. At a loss to explain what he was looking at, the coroner decided to list the cause of death as suicide.

Hunter Mortley
Albuquerque, NM

Frozen on the River

My dad used to tell me this story when I was growing up in Las Vegas, New Mexico back in the 1950s.

It seems that a woman was married to a man that drank too much – a *borracho*. He would come home late at night from the bar and he would start pushing her around, hitting her and yelling at her. She had two little children and she began to be afraid that he might hurt them.

So, one night, when he was out drinking, she took the children down to the river where Bridge Street is now, and put them under the bridge there. She told them to be quiet and to wait for her and that she would return very soon. Then she went home to gather her things and to pack up and leave her husband for good. She had decided that she could not spend another night under the same roof with this man.

Well, it was a very cold night, and she took too long. Who knows why? Maybe she had to feed the horses before she left. Maybe someone came by to visit and she had to pass the time a little bit by sharing some gossip – what we call *platicando*. Anyway, when she finally got back to the bridge, the children had frozen to death.

That was *La Llorona*. To this day, she walks the riverbed in Las Vegas, crying and weeping for her children.

Robert V. Montoya
Las Vegas, NM

The Musicians that Played for La Llorona

In a little town in Mexico, there lived a *campesino* – a farmer – named Felipe Cabezón, which incidentally means "big-headed." This is a story of what occurred when he was a young man of twenty-two.

Ever since Felipe was a *niño* he had dreamed of being a famous orchestra leader. Because of this, seven members of his *familia* decided to work and save their money so that they could purchase little Felipe a violin. His brother José would exhaust his two burros carrying firewood to sell in town, and his twin sisters María and Miguela would make *tortillas de maiz* to sell to the *ricos* – the rich people – in the surrounding countryside. No matter how tired they were, they always reminded each other, "Someday Felipe will make us all proud." To ensure his future, they also hired a teacher, Señor Luis Ramirez from Celaya, who would give him weekly violin lessons.

There was one problem, however. Felipe was a little lazy. Even though El Señor Ramirez would faithfully appear at the door of the Cabezón family's humble home every Tuesday evening to work with the little boy for one hour, neither he nor anyone else could seem to convince little Felipe that it was necessary to *practicar, practicar, y practicar!* Indeed, Felipe would pick up his bow and violin only once or twice after El Señor Ramirez would leave, but would soon put them down and find something else to do that was more interesting – like staring out the kitchen window and dreaming of being rich and famous without working too hard for it.

By the time Felipe had become an adult, he had broken his family's hearts. Señor Ramirez was long gone after sitting down with the family one evening when Felipe was thirteen and telling them, "The money you give me is like water down a drain. The boy is not interested and never will be. *Es muy vago* – he is very lazy."

Shortly after he turned twenty-two, Felipe was reading the newspaper and saw an advertisement that said, "Musicians to play at the midnight dance. Good pay." Felipe said to himself, "This is what I have been waiting for. This will launch my career as an orchestra conductor." Since his abilities with the violin were amateur at best, Felipe knew that he would simply lead the musicians with a little baton and then be paid handsomely for it. With that in mind, he rushed to the telephone to call the number in the advertisement. To his surprise, the person who answered told him, *"Eres el unico que a llamado* – you are the only person that has called." Realizing that he had a short time to get a group together, Felipe searched the countryside and found two guitarists, a trumpeter and a drummer, all self-taught musicians who quickly agreed to join his band. They spent the next few days and nights rehearsing frantically, keeping the entire neighborhood up half the night.

Soon, the big day arrived. The five men started out early and walked to the address that Felipe had been given, arriving an hour later at the front of a beautiful mansion. "How strange," one of them said, "that in this alley once called *El Camino de las Animas* – the road of the souls – one would find such an elegant home." "I have never seen this home," exclaimed the trumpeter. "Neither have I," one of the guitarists said, "and I have lived here all my life."

A servant opened the door for them, which creaked loudly. The little band of musicians stepped into a large ballroom furnished luxuriously with beautiful tile floors and thick drapes on all the doors and windows. Huge ornate mirrors graced the high walls and colorful flowers were everywhere. The musicians could not get over their amazement as they sat down in seats that had been reserved for them. The servant said, *"El patrón quiere que tocan un vals* – the master wishes you to play a waltz." Although the ballroom was empty, the men stood and began to play, with Felipe waving his baton up and down when he thought he should, already counting the money in his head. From two doors at the end of the great room, couples began to arrive and dance together. Even though the room was very luxurious, the lighting was poor and it was dark in many areas of the room. The dancers kept coming, and now it seemed that they were coming through doors that hadn't existed before. Soon, the room was filled with dancing couples as the musicians played on and on.

Then one of the musicians remarked in shock, *"Dios mio* – look at their feet!!" All the musicians' eyes were directed at once toward the floor and to a hundred pairs of goat hooves. "And the ladies don't seem to have eyes," said one of the musicians, now trembling with fear and struggling to continue playing his guitar. "Yes, the ladies have eyes," responded another, "but they glow red when the light hits them!" As the musicians became increasingly aware of their surroundings, they realized that the great mirrors on the wall reflected a completely empty room.

The musicians had seen enough. As they grabbed their instruments and prepared to leave, one of the female dancers stepped out from the shadows and approached them. Her head was covered with a black lace *mantilla* that fell down around her shoulders and she wore a long black dress. "Hello, Felipe," she said, in a low voice. "Perhaps you remember me." Felipe, being the coward that he was, tried to duck behind Lazaro, the guitarist. He tried to keep his voice from shaking. "I – I don't remember you. Who are you?"

"That surprises me," she responded, "because I have been following you since you were a little boy. When you go down to the river to fish, I am always there on the other side, watching you and weeping. When you walk through the arroyos on your way to the field, I am right behind you, crying and wailing. Surely you know who I am, Felipe?" she asked. "Do you not know *La Llorona*?" She pulled back her veil, revealing her face for the first time, her red eyes glowing as the light hit them, her mouth a black hole.

Felipe opened his mouth to scream. But just then, a male figure stepped out from the shadows and walked up to Felipe, who found himself looking right into the face of his old violin teacher, Señor Ramirez, who said to him, "Do you not realize that you are in Hell? And that *La Llorona* is here to claim you, her lost child?" At that moment, she reached out to Felipe with her bony long fingers and pulled him toward her as his ears were filled with her horrible weeping and screaming. This was his last memory. As for the four musicians, they saw all they needed to. They dropped their instruments and ran out the front door. As they turned around to look at the mansion they had just left, it had mysteriously disappeared.

And what no one could explain was that a leather pouch full of money had been placed outside the front door of the Cabezón family home the next morning. When Felipe's mother and father counted the bills, it came to the exact amount that they had paid Señor Ramirez for all of Felipe's violin lessons over the years.

Marco Luis Torres
Guanajuato, Mexico

The Veil in the Road

I grew up in Fort Garland, Colorado. There were seven of us kids in our little house, and I was the second oldest. My four brothers shared one bedroom and my two sisters and I shared another one. It was my job to take care of everyone while my parents were working. Fort Garland is in the San Luis Valley, which I guess you could say was a hotbed of *La Llorona* stories – everyone knew somebody who had seen her or experienced her personally, and many of the stories about her were hair-raising. The terrible story I am about to relate haunts me to this day.

In August of 1963, when I was seventeen, there was a wedding dance in Fort Garland at a friend's house that I had been looking forward to for weeks. I had my dress picked out and my shoes picked out. All my friends were going, and my favorite band would be playing. A bunch of friends were coming by to pick me up, and my brother Rudy was going with a group of friends from his class. Everything was fine until about an hour before it was time to leave. Rudy and I were sitting in the kitchen finishing up dinner when my mom suddenly announced to us, "I don't want you kids going to that dance. I've got a funny feeling about it and I can't explain it. So you're not going."

It felt like the floor had caved in under my feet. I was prone to dramatics at that age, and so I got kind of hysterical about it after my mom dug in her heels and said her decision was final. Rudy, on the other hand, had a completely different reaction. He said he was going anyway. I ran to my room and threw myself on the bed. I can still remember the sound of Rudy's friends driving up and hearing the front door close as Rudy left. I cried myself to sleep, furious at Rudy for defying our mom and furious at myself for not having the nerve to defy her, too.

Several hours later, my mom came into the room and shook me awake. She snapped on the light next to my bed. It was still dark. "Wake up, Lydia!" she cried, "Your brother just came home and something terrible has happened."

My brother was sitting in the living room on the couch, his head in his hands. He looked up at me. "Lydia, your friends. They're all gone. They're dead."

It was three days before I could think straight, but here is what happened. Rudy told us that, on the way back from the wedding dance, the car ahead of him on the highway, the one with my friends, had suddenly braked after driving at highway speed and gone off the road. The car Rudy was in swerved to avoid it. The wreck was terrible. Cars didn't have seatbelts back then, so everyone was thrown out of the car when it flipped over.

According to the police report, a crying woman in a long black dress with a veil over her face had crossed the highway in front of the first car. Later that night, the police found a black veil on the pavement not far from the wreckage.

To this day, I wonder if it was true that it was *La Llorona* who caused the accident. My brother's friend, the one who was driving, swore up and down that it was true; that he saw her with his own eyes. If that's true, then *La Llorona* is still out there, haunting the highways of the San Luis Valley -- because she never dies.

Lydia Ortiz Avant
Fort Garland, Colorado

An Opportunity Missed

I was born and raised on Santa Fe's west side, the real heart of this town. My father's side of the family came from Lincoln County, which was Billy the Kid country; in fact, my great-great uncle, James Brent, was Pat Garrett's deputy and his son William wrote a book about the Kid. Schutz is a Czech name, but we all consider ourselves to be part of *La Raza* – the Spanish people.

I grew up always conscious of *La Llorona*. I guess all of us kids were back then. Since the Santa Fe River runs through the heart of the west side, and there were so many stories about people who had seen her or heard her over the years in that part of town, it was second nature to keep an eye out for her.

One morning in 1965, when I was about fifteen years old, I was driving north to work on St. Francis Drive, one of the main streets here. Because it was so early, the streets were completely deserted – there wasn't a soul anywhere. The sun had just come up and it was very beautiful and still. As I was driving along, I got to the corner of St. Francis and Alameda and stopped for the red light. The southeast side of that corner is where Luther Chavez' welding yard was, and his house faced the Santa Fe River. As I sat there waiting for the light to change, something caught the corner of my eye and I found myself suddenly looking over toward Luther's place and the little bridge right near his house. And lo and behold, there she was!

I remember to this day what she looked like. I will never forget the sight, because she was so striking: She was completely dressed in black, with waist-length salt-and-pepper hair. She was a *viejita* – a little old lady – at least seventy-five or eighty years old, but what does a kid of fifteen know? She was elderly. I said to myself, "What is that person doing out here on that bridge at this hour of the morning?" But it was much more than that. Santa Fe was still a very small town in those days, and I knew everyone in that neighborhood. I had never seen this person before, and somehow knew that I never would again. I knew that I was looking at something supernatural – *un espiritu* – something that was not of this world. How did I know that? I don't know. Maybe I can put it this way: You don't usually look at a person and feel like you've been struck by lightning, yet this is how I felt when I saw this old lady. If you asked me if she had an aura, I'd have to tell you that I've never seen an aura. But they say people see auras in their subconscious minds, and that's why people are repelled by some people and attracted by others. In this case, I couldn't take my eyes away from her.

As I sat there in my car, feeling almost frozen, she turned and looked at me. At that exact moment, the light turned green and I found myself automatically driving off without a second thought. A few seconds later I said to myself, "Wait a minute, what am I doing?" I did a U-turn and raced back to the spot.

She was gone by the time I got there. For someone to disappear that quickly from that particular spot was impossible -- unless she had jumped into the river. My heart sank because I felt I had missed a great opportunity to see her up close and maybe even talk to her!

Later that day, I told my mother about the incident. She said, "That must have been *La Llorona*." In the course of the next week or two, I told most of my friends about it. And whenever I was near the original sighting, I'd kind of keep my eye out for her. I never did find her, and I knew deep down I never would.

There was a reason for *La Llorona* appearing to me that day, and I truly believe there was a message for me in it. But I blew it when I decided to drive off without investigating it further. And I regret it to this day.

David Schutz
Santa Fe, NM

Face to Face with La Llorona

This encounter took place in Parral, Mexico. It was 1897, almost the turn of the century, when my grandmother's grandfather had an encounter with the infamous *La Llorona*. His name was Miguel Romero. He was only ten years old when this happened.

It was a hot night in July. Miguel couldn't sleep, so he went out to talk to the town crier, Señor Olivas. They had town criers in those days that yelled out the time twenty-four hours a day. Nobody was afraid to go out at night because it was safer back then. Anyway, Miguel was talking to Señor Olivas, when out of nowhere a lady in a long white dress that was draped around her body came toward them. She asked the time in a whimpering voice, like she was crying. When Miguel and Señor Olivas looked at her, they noticed that her face was that of a skeleton, with very big holes where the eyes were, and her mouth was like a big black hole, but shaped like an oval. Inside the oval they could see tiny white things that looked like teeth at first, but then they saw that they were not teeth, they were a whole bunch of tiny little *lloronas* in white, just like the big one that was standing in front of them. Very frightened by what he saw, Señor Olivas stood frozen, like his legs were paralyzed. Then, just like that, the lady was lifted up into the sky by an unknown force. She looked like a huge white bird. Then they heard a loud, shrieking, blood-curling cry: *"Donde estan mis hijos!!* – Where are my children!! – and then she faded out of sight.

Señor Olivas refused to speak of this horrible experience again, but Miguel told this story to anyone who would listen. He swore until the day he died sixty-two years later that the mysterious lady was *La Llorona*.

Claudia Martinez
El Paso, Texas

The Widow Named Maria

Here in Guatemala, there are many stories about *La Llorona*. This is one that is popular in my area of Quetzaltenango, which is Guatemala's second largest city.

Many, many years ago in ancient Guatemala, by the *Rio Pensativo* – the river of thoughtfulness and meditation – there lived a beautiful widow named Maria. She had a son, Adan, whom she loved with all her soul. He was her only companion. The ladies of the village did not like her, however, because she was so beautiful that they thought she would take their husbands away from them. But as the saying goes, *el malo siempre piensa engaño* – the evil thought always deceives you – and none of these ladies ever went near her or tried to be her friend. That was too bad, because Maria was a very kindhearted and gentle soul who would have proved to be a loyal friend to any of these other ladies.

Maria used to like to go out in the early evenings on strolls with her young son. He was a typical little boy – as soon as he saw his friends come near, he would join them to play by the side of the river. Maria would watch Adan run to join his friends, and her heart would fill with joy as she thought to herself how very much this child meant to her.

One morning, Maria tried to get out of bed but found that she was feeling quite ill. Her condition was such that the only reason she would get up was to feed Adan. The next day, though, her health began to improve a little bit and so she got out of bed to clean up the house while Adan went out to play with his friends by the side of the river. It had rained heavily earlier that day, and the river was at the flood stage. While Maria was cleaning the house, she suddenly heard some excited voices from outside the house, and she ran outside to see what the commotion was about. There she met up with a group of neighbors who were coming over to tell her that the floodwaters had swept her son away. Maria started to wail and cry, "*No es verdad lo que dice la gente!* – It is not true what the people are saying!" – and in desperation she ran towards the river crying out, "*Ayyyyy miii hiiiiijoooo* – Oh, my son!"

After that day, Maria's house was abandoned and she disappeared. No smoke was seen coming from her chimney ever again. For the first time, the jealous neighbors felt tranquility in their hearts because the woman who could have taken their husbands away was now gone forever.

They say that Maria's suffering has not ended, and that even today one can hear her crying along the banks of the *Rio Pensativo*. The neighbors from the little village say they often hear her terrible agonizing cries, the same cry that was heard the day her son disappeared -- *Ayyyyy miii hiiiiijoooo* – and they say it is the cry of *La Llorona*.

Manuel S. Oliva
Quetzaltenango, Guatemala

The Haunting of Pojoaque

When I was nine years old — this was in 1946 — we moved from Santa Fe to Pojoaque. My parents weren't religious, so I hadn't gone to church a whole lot, but the whole Pojoaque community in those days was involved in the old church, which was up on the hill by the Pojoaque Pueblo. It's been torn down since then and a new church has been built, but at the time it was an old, old church. A beautiful one, I thought – I could never understand why anyone would want to tear it down. It had an ornate altar painted with the *santos* and the *angels* – something I had never experienced in my life. When somebody died, we'd go to the funeral there so we didn't have to go to school. That way, we never ditched school, so to speak. All my friends were Spanish. I was the only Anglo.

I don't remember what day it was, but the saint's day that church was named after was a big day for everyone in the Pojoaque community. There would be a high Mass and a parade, and the priest would have his incense burner and he would sprinkle the ground around the church with holy water. Then a procession would follow, around and around the church, with banners and so on. It was very elaborate and awe-inspiring. The old-timers would have blunderbusses and would load them with black powder and shoot them in the air and this smoke would go all over – boom, boom! This would go on all day.

Toward evening, the women would bring food, some of them traveling with horses and wagons, and then the *luminarias* – crisscrossed split logs of piñon piled in a square -- would be lit. The Indians would come too, since the pueblo was right there. In fact, during the procession around the church, they would beat on drums. It was really, really something. I loved to go because there were so many kids running around. So when they lit the *luminarias* that night, everyone sat around and started telling stories like: "Don't go into the graveyard at night because the dead people will pull your toes." Or: "If you hear an owl hoot, it means the dead are rising out of their graves."

Anyway, we were running all over the place, the way kids do. Of course, we never went near the cemetery, but we were playing around near the cottonwoods by the river, and an owl started hooting. There were about seven of us kids, and we all stopped to listen to the owl because we thought it was the dead rising. We were very quiet, listening to the owl, when all of a sudden we started hearing some other kind of crying. We looked around, and I'll never forget this: The smoke from the fires had drifted down to the river, the way smoke travels toward a river and settles down in there, and there she was, illuminated in smoke. The lady in black with the veil, and all that. And she was crying, and she walked into the cemetery and then she just walked around in there, crying in a sad and plaintive voice. It scared us terribly, and we took off and ran back to the area where the *luminarias* were, where there was light, and it was then that they told us the story of *La Llorona*.

The story was about a woman named Enriqueta Gomez y Lujan. In the olden days, the Ute Indians had come out of Colorado and taken her twin boys and killed them both down by the river. They had buried them in that cemetery where the church was, and since that time she had been coming there, crying and searching for them among the graves.

Stephen W. Long
Albuquerque, New Mexico

The "R" Car to
Tortilla Flats

I lived in East Los Angeles during the 1940s – on South Fresno Street, to be exact, right across from the White Fence area – so I consider myself to be a bit knowledgeable about the *pachuco* era. It is believed that the term originated from the word *pocho,* which refers to a Native-born Californian of Spanish descent.

The *pachuco* style of dress was very distinctive, and grooming was fastidious. The cuffs on the pants were called "ankle chokers." The pants were very baggy – in fact, at the knees, the material was almost three yards wide. They were "Dutch-pressed" into two pleats, one in the front and one on the side. The shoes, which were highly polished wingtips, had soles nearly two inches thick. Of course, the hair was greased into an elaborate ducktail. Some *pachucos* also had an "inaugural cross" tattooed on their foreheads between the eyebrows, while others had the cross on their right hand between the thumb and index finger. In later years, I had a rose tattooed over the cross on my hand. My cousin Bobby had the cross on his forehead professionally removed by a doctor.

The Anglos and Blacks used to imitate the *pachuco* style of dress. They called themselves "Zoot suiters." The most popular material for these suits was sharkskin, which was shiny and looked very classy.

My stepfather hated this style of dress. He used to take my shoes to the shoe repair shop and have the soles removed, and a few weeks later I'd just go back and have new ones nailed on. It was a constant tug of war between us. I wasn't the only one, though – a lot of the *plebe* – the other guys – had the same problem with their dads.

The Hispanics of East Los Angeles, like the Hispanics everywhere else, all knew about *La Llorona*. Richard Morales and his kid brother Nacho claim that they used to see her almost every Friday night, usually around fifteen or twenty minutes past midnight, after they left the late show at the Crystal Movie Theater on Whittier Boulevard. They would see her riding the "R" car, which was a trolley that ran up 7th on Whittier to Indiana Street. She always seemed to be sitting alone in the back of the trolley car, so the story goes, and it was easy to spot her because the inside was extremely well lit. They insisted it was *La Llorona* because she always appeared in the same car at the same time, every Friday night like clockwork, and some people who saw her claimed that she would suddenly vaporize.

David Gonzales, a friend of mine who tried to be a *pachuco* but could never really carry it off because his dad was too strict, said he spotted *La Llorona* walking on South Fresno Street toward Euclid Avenue one Friday evening. Many of the *pachucos* of that day were constantly looking for her, checking out 38th Street, *La Washington,* California Street, the whole city, in fact. I have to admit that I never saw her myself.

The old-timers used to see her a lot more often. They said it was because they were believers, while us younger kids were not.

Eduardo Garcia Kraul
Santa Fe, NM

The Horse That Left No Tracks

La Llorona used to haunt the travelers coming into the La Joya and Pecos areas from Rowe back in the 1870s. This was before New Mexico was a state and they called it the New Mexico Territory. My *visabuelo* – my great grandfather – told me the following story of his experience in those days:

"We were on the way to Santa Fe in the old covered wagon, and it was a little before dusk when we arrived in the La Joya area. I was traveling with your father and your great grandmother, Ramoncita. It was early summer and there had been a sudden and heavy rain. The air was still damp and smelled very beautiful. The *cedros* – the juniper trees – were still glistening with the raindrops and the air was so clear you could see the pale gold of the *muerdago*, what you call mistletoe, weighing down the branches.

"We had stopped for a few minutes to eat some food we had brought with us, when we saw in the distance a lady riding a white horse with her *tapalo*, her shawl, floating behind her. She was galloping very fast and coming directly toward us. There was something ghostly and unnatural about her, like something from another world. We thought of the stories we had heard about *La Llorona* on the white horse, which was very popular at the time, and chills ran up my spine. I told your father and my Ramoncita, 'Let's get inside the wagon and close the flaps until she goes by.' We threw our food into the back and climbed in as quickly as we could. The flaps were not very good; they were tattered and frayed from the weather and we had to hold them closed. As we huddled inside, we heard her approach, dismount, and walk around the wagon as though she were inspecting it. We were very frightened. Then we heard her mount her horse and ride off. We still waited a long time before we decided that it was safe to look out. To us it seemed like forever! We climbed out of the wagon and, upon looking around, we saw her footprints, but for all the searching we did we could not find the hoof prints of the horse. The sand was still wet and untouched after the storm.

"There are people that claim *La Llorona* was a very beautiful woman with jet black hair and a very suntanned complexion."

Carlos Valdez
Española, NM

The Test Drive

I was a miner in the 1930s and was living in Raton around that time. In those days, nearly everyone in town was involved in the coal mining operations of the area in one way or the other. There wasn't much of a reason to live there unless you mined or maybe raised a little cattle.

I used to spend many hours in the *cantinas* – those were rough days and we used to swap a lot of stories to pass the time. There was a bartender, Romero, who told me this story and even as I tell it to you now, it gives me the willies.

Seems that this fella placed an ad in the Raton Range, I believe it was, during the years of the Great Depression, to sell his Model T car for a hundred dollars. The advertisement ran a long time and there were no takers until one hot summer day when a woman called and expressed a real interest in seeing his car and taking it for a test drive. This was unusual – a woman calling a man to make a business transaction of that sort in those days, but the little lady sounded real determined and he sure as hell needed the money.

So he arranged to meet her down by the railroad tracks at seven-thirty that evening, and when he got there, a woman in a black, heavy cloak was waiting for him. The sun was about to set, but it was still very, very warm and there she was, dressed for winter. She indicated to him that she would crank the car up, and after she did, she motioned for him to move over to the passenger's side so she could drive. Then she hopped in like she really knew her business and took off like a bat out of hell, if you'll excuse the expression. They were going very fast on the dirt road, twenty or twenty-five miles an hour, and after about ten minutes or so of this, he turned to her and asked, "Lady, just where do you think you're going? This is just a test drive." She didn't answer him. He even mentioned to her that he was starting to feel a little green around the gills with all the bouncing around, but he may as well have been talking to himself for all the response he got.

After a time, the car began to get very cold inside, and then the sun set, and still they kept going. It was like a dream, almost, where a person has no sense of time or place. A few times he wanted to just holler, "Stop the car," or throw the door open and jump out, but he couldn't do nothing but stare like a zombie through the windshield like he was paralyzed. And the car was getting colder and colder inside.

Now, this fella was also a veteran of the trenches in World War I and so he had a real good sense of survival. He knew there was something real peculiar happening, and he decided to just sit tight and be quiet and not fight this feeling that had come over him of being paralyzed. He figured to himself that if he got out of this situation in one piece, he'd buy everybody back at the bar a drink or two.

Anyway, the road started to get a lot rougher and they were bouncing around like a couple of Mexican jumping beans on a hot plate. Finally, it seemed like they hit sand and then they were going down a hill of sorts. The sand got deeper and deeper, and the car began to get bogged down, and then the wheels started spinning and pretty soon they stopped turning completely. So they just sat there for a while. It was deadly quiet outside as well as inside. No crickets, no frogs, no coyotes, nothing. You could have heard an egg frying at a hundred yards.

After about an eternity or so, the lady turned to this fella for the first time and in this deep watery voice that seemed to come from the bottom of a well, she snarled, "I'll take the car. You get out. *Now!*" Then she pushed one of those little Bull Durham tobacco bags into his hands. It was full of paper and coins, but it felt more like ice cubes. At that exact second, his strength shot back into his body and he threw the car door open and ran as fast as he could into the night. As he was running from the riverbed, scrambling up the sandy sides of the arroyo, he could hear her voice follow him, rising into a blood-curdling wail that echoed everywhere.

He got a ride with some people back to Raton. They told him that he wasn't far from the town of Chico. After he described the woman to various folks in the course of the next few days, someone said to him, "That's *La Llorona.* She goes down to that particular riverbed a lot. That's the first time, though, that she's used a car to get there." This fella supposedly moved out of Raton right after that incident and settled in San Antonio.

Waylon Tuttle
Tulsa, OK

La Llorona the Vampire

My father came from Puebla de Zaragoza, capital of the state of Puebla in Mexico. He was an ironworker and used to make ornamental designs for doors and windows. He even shoed horses. He always wanted to be an engineer on the railroad and to pilot a train himself. His chance came in the early 1940s when the U.S. government signed an agreement with Mexico that allowed them to recruit laborers to work on the railroad in the U.S. These laborers were called *braceros,* meaning people who work with their arms. These *braceros* worked any job they could get – picking fruit, laying rails, even butchering. Hundreds of Mexicans were recruited by the big meat packing plants in Wichita, Kansas – Cudahy, Swift and Armour – to do butchering during the First World War when there was a shortage of labor there. Today, their descendants make up a large part of the Latino community in Wichita.

So to get back to my dad, he came to *El Norte* and traveled to Kansas and started work laying track for the railroad. As you may know, the city of Leavenworth is situated on the west bank of the Missouri River and the Mexican people there were always reporting that *La Llorona* was wandering up and down the banks of this river. Dad never paid much attention to these stories until early one summer evening that just happened to fall on a Friday the 13th. It was about seven-thirty and the men were laying track on the spur of the railroad around the area of the Santa Fe Trail, when a fellow by the name of Fernando "Chalano" Para looked toward the setting sun and called across the track to my dad, *"Quien no es el chino que biene gritando y corriendo para este rumbo?* – Is that not Mr. Chan, the Chinese gentleman, running in this direction and hollering?" Well, it was.

Mr. Chan ran up to them and stammered, "She said she is *La Llorona!*" He was babbling like a baby and his knees were shaking so hard he could barely stand up. My dad said that he was as white as a *gringo.* A little crowd formed around him right away. Everyone was very curious, because here was an eyewitness at last and not just someone saying, "I know someone who knows someone whose cousin saw *La Llorona.*" So they gave Mr. Chan some sips of wine and waited until he calmed down.

After they lit a fire and the sun had set, Mr. Chan told the others that, right after he quit work and was headed south back to the camp, out of nowhere a tall lady in white flowing robes with the face of a vampire appeared in his path. She said to him, "Today, I, *La Llorona,* will drink your blood."

Now, what was interesting about this story was that it was the first time anyone could remember that a person without any Mexican or Spanish blood had actually seen *La Llorona.* People thought, just as they do now, that you had to believe in her in order to see her, so in this case, I guess even the Chinese people believe in her!

My dad's wish came true, by the way. He did manage to pilot a train, to be an engineer and to become a member of the Brotherhood of Locomotive Firemen and Engine Men, and to work his way from being a peasant *bracero* to an employee of a Class L railroad. This goes to prove that even a poor Mexican peasant can work his way up to be somebody here in the great United States of America.

R. Miranda
Henderson, NV

46

The Haunting of Placita Rafaela

The story goes that a Mr. Garcia decided to visit Paul's Lounge here in Santa Fe one Good Friday, even though his wife begged him not to because she was afraid he would be cursed for it. He went anyway, and drank there all day long. By the time he left that night, he was pretty well inebriated. He started walking home through Tenorio Street, and as he neared Garcia Street where it turns into Acequia Madre, he heard someone crying. He turned and saw a woman shrouded completely in white, standing in the moonlight and pointing at him. Terrified, he ran up the Acequia Madre to where Tito's Market used to be, and fell down there in the street. By the time he got up and dusted himself off, she was gone.

As he turned down Placita Rafaela, he saw a little baby lying in the middle of his driveway, wrapped in a white blanket and crying pitifully. He walked over and picked it up, wondering whose baby this was and why it was there in the middle of the night. Noticing that its face was covered with a blanket, he opened it to look and there she was, a baby-sized *La Llorona*, starting at him with her big, dark penetrating eyes and her sharp white teeth and her big, ugly, bony hand pointing at him. He dropped the bundle and ran into the house, and he hasn't had a drink since that night.

Phil Griego
Santa Fe, NM

Ralph Martinez' Long Ride Home

My family has been in the Santa Fe area for more than 150 years. My father, Abel Dominguez, was from Tesuque, born in 1894, and my grandpa used to own the Bishops Lodge properties.

In 1949, Ralph Martinez was a projectionist at the Paris Theater, which was on San Francisco Street two blocks from where the Lensic Theater is now. One night, he was riding his bike home after running the movie projector through a double horror feature – I remember one of the movies was "Frankenstein Meets the Wolf Man," and the other one was a Dracula movie – and he came upon a lady on Magdalena Lane who was only three or four feet tall, with scraggly hair. She started this terrible moaning and crying as soon as she saw him, wringing her hands and wailing something terrible in this high-pitched, deafening scream. She had a wrinkly little face and a long ugly nose covered with little warts.

It scared the pants off Ralph, so he just dropped his bike on the spot and ran to the Visarraga home, where they let him spend the rest of the night. The next day, he took a bunch of us guys to go get his bike. We found it on the side of the road right where he said he left it. To the day he died, Ralph swore up and down it was *La Llorona*.

Juan Dominguez
Santa Fe, NM

El Molino

In 1925 here in Santa Fe, where Sosaya Lane meets Acequia Madre, our *primo* Ramon Vigil had a *molenito* – a small mill – and he used to grind the corn for the people. Every ten sacks he ground for you, you gave him one sack in payment. The wheels of the mill were constantly turning. He was very, very busy. People ate a lot of corn tortillas in those days.

If you walked by the mill at night, you could hear the creaking and groaning of the wheels, and we used to get the chills listening to it. It was said that *La Llorona* would appear and that her crying would mingle with the noise of the wheels grinding the corn late at night. You wouldn't know it was her, though, until you were practically standing next to her. My *primo* said that he ran into her one night and she had skin like leather and her eyes glowed in the dark like a cat, but they were reddish in color.

When us kids walked by the mill at night, we would say a whole rosary in just half a block!

Alfonso "Trompo" Trujillo
Santa Fe, NM

Lassoing La Llorona

I used to be Deputy Chief of the New Mexico State Police. I retired in 1985. When I was growing up, my father, Celso Chavez, who is now deceased, used to tell us stories about things he had witnessed in his younger days. One of the most interesting stories he told us was that, one lonely night many years ago, as he was riding his horse from El Coyote to Guadalupita, he observed a *bulto*—a form—near the local cemetery that looked like someone dressed in dark clothing. He could not see its face because it was covered with what looked like a *tapalo*—a shawl. At that point, my father decided to try and lasso this *bulto,* as he had heard so much about *La Llorona* and he figured, "This must be her." The *bulto* was eighty to a hundred feet away, but he couldn't get his horse to run fast enough; he said it was scared and kept rearing back and seemed reluctant to pursue it. So the *bulto* disappeared out of sight.

My father had a lot of guts and was never afraid of anything, so I can see that he wanted to satisfy himself as to what this *bulto* was.

T.J. Chavez
Santa Fe, NM

La Llorona Gets Shot

I was born in 1906 in a very old adobe house – it was considered old even then – on my dad's ranch, which was right on the river in the El Macho area of Pecos, New Mexico. My mother was Rosita Gallegos; my father, Agapito Cortez. I worked in the mines for twenty-seven years, both hard rock and coal mines, in Madrid and Santa Rita, New Mexico, and in Montana, Idaho, and Washington. After that, I went to work in the Chicago post office. I've got black lung now, and I have to have oxygen. I have a sign on my door that says: "Lungs at Work: No Smoking." Believe it or not, if I didn't have it there, some people wouldn't think twice about lighting up a cigarette in my living room. You could blow up the whole place, you know.

My dad was a mail carrier in Pecos, and he delivered the mail on horseback. He always carried a .44 pistol. You never knew in those days who you might run into.

In 1904, there was a terrible flood in Pecos that washed away many houses and some bridges. It lasted for several days and many people had to leave their houses and stay with family members who were lucky enough not to live so close to the river.

My father was delivering the mail during this time in an area called Peñasco Alto, which means "high rocky place," right above Juanita Byrd's ranch in a neighborhood called Encinoso. They called it that because it was full of oak trees. Now it's called the Hidden Valley Ranch. It's a very beautiful spot. *La Llorona* used to cry and wail around there. People heard her many times; they said she was a phantom dressed in black who wandered among the rocks and juniper trees.

One winter night after the flooding began, my father was traveling through that area on his horse when he heard the terrible wailing and crying of *La Llorona*. It was so close, no more than ten or fifteen feet away, that he got out his .44 and fired it toward the source of the sound. The blood-curdling cries stopped almost immediately, and no one ever heard the sound of *La Llorona* again in that particular spot.

My relations, Guadalupe and Porfiria Gonzales, used to tell this story to many others. It was one of the first stories I heard as a child. More than eighty years have passed and I still remember it very well.

Victor Cortez
Santa Fe, NM

The Hippie Learns a Lesson

There are many stories here in Chimayó about *La Llorona*. This is one of my favorites.

Back about 1970, the first hippies moved here. Some of them were okay, but some of them were very disrespectful. This story concerns one of the disrespectful ones, who was also a thief.

This hippie was named after some animal or bird – the hippies used names like that. He was named "Bear," or "Crow." Maybe it was "Mole." Okay, so Mole had a wife who also had a strange name like "Sunshine" or "Ocean," and they had a couple of kids who ran around with runny noses and no pants or shoes. They bought a little piece of land that no one else would want and built a house that was all underground, with boards over the top for a roof. My husband and I thought it was a terrible place to live.

Now, Mole was from California and had a very rich family, so he never had to work and he didn't have any respect for people who worked hard.

The first trouble we had with Mole was when he would go riding horses across our pasture and leave the gates open so the cows would get out. My poor husband would spend days chasing them back into the pasture. This caused a lot of trouble for us, believe me. A couple of people even shot in his direction, but he didn't pay any attention. He thought the land belonged to everyone and there shouldn't be any fences, but my husband says, "Good fences make good neighbors."

The other thing we all thought was strange was that this hippie had some idea he was an Indian. We would see him riding his horse along the arroyo and all he wore was this little leather thing like Tarzan, with beads and feathers around his neck and moccasins.

The neighbors tried to ignore Mole, but soon they started to notice signs that something had been in their gardens. At first it was like the skunks do when they get at the corn with all the ears broken off. Then, other vegetables started to disappear and some fruit, too. We soon realized it wasn't a skunk – not the four-legged kind, anyway.

Nobody had caught this Mole stealing, but people knew it was him anyway. It went on through the summer, and then, that fall, in October, it all stopped. We had a long summer that year with no frost in September, so there was still food in many gardens. One of the best gardens belonged to Mrs. Martinez and she told me this story.

Late one night in this particular October, when the moon was almost full and the leaves were dry and rustling on the trees, Mrs. Martinez could not sleep. She had sciatica, *pobrecita,* so she was up at her table late, drinking *atole* and looking out the window. Hearing a noise, she looked closer and saw this hippie Mole in her garden with a sack and all of a sudden she realized he was taking her carrots! He was wearing his Tarzan costume and had smeared himself with mud so he couldn't be seen.

The wind was blowing that night, so there were noises from the loose tin on Mrs. Martinez's roof and the tree branches. Now, it happens that Mrs. Martinez's garden is right below the Martinez *acequia,* which is the big one that runs through the plaza, and it is well known that *La Llorona* likes the ditches.

So, as Mrs. Martinez was watching this Mole person through her window, she heard the wind really start to howl louder and louder. Then she realized that it was not just the wind – it was the cry of *La Llorona!* At that moment, she saw Mole straighten up all of a sudden after bending over the carrot patch, and even through the mud on his face, she could see his eyes get big. Across the ditch came floating *La Llorona,* tall like she is, and all dressed in black, increasing her howling by the minute. Mole dropped the sack of carrots and began to run, He was so scared he ran right into the fence and fell down. He tried to get up, but his body failed him and so he scrambled along on all fours.

All along the road, as Mole ran, the howling continued and all the porch lights came on and the dogs began to bark. Everyone saw Mole, running as fast as he could, his Indian braids standing out straight behind him as he ran for his life.

After that night, Mole took his family to live somewhere else. He is probably still stealing because, as the saying goes, *"La zorra mudara los dientes pero no las mientes* – The fox may lose its teeth but not its ways."

But, thanks to *La Llorona,* this doesn't happen in our village anymore.

Refugio Archuleta
Chimayó, NM

The Mystery of Ramona Sena

My uncle told me that this incident happened up in the *milpas,* the gardening areas of Cerro Gordo in Santa Fe, in the 1700s. This is a true story that has been passed down through the generations in my own family.

A woman, Valentina, had been working in the gardens picking corn and squash, and she had set her baby down under a tree while she worked. It was her first day on the job and she was new to the area, having come down from Tierra Amarilla a few days before. It was late summer and very beautiful. The crops were especially plentiful that particular year, and many farmers were using extra workers from wherever they could find them.

Later in the day, the *patron* sent a message from his house that he wanted to see her, so Valentina asked one of the other women, also a new worker by the name of Ramona Sena, to watch the baby while she walked the mile or so to the *patron's* house on Cerro Gordo. She walked quickly, and arrived only moments before a violent rainstorm came on.

A while later, all of the workers appeared in front of the house because it did not appear that the rain would stop and they could no longer work in the downpour. Valentina looked out the window at the little group of people, and then ran to the door asking, "Where is Ramona Sena who was caring for my baby?" The people looked at each other and then said, "Ramona? No one has seen her for the past year or so." Valentina broke away from the group and ran in the pouring rain back to the *milpas*. She could not find Ramona or her baby.

To this day, they say it was *La Llorona* who had taken on the form of Ramona Sena. No one has seen Ramona Sena since, and the baby was never found.

Many of the old-timers say that *La Llorona* takes on different forms of women to confuse and frighten people, while at other times she does it to help people.

John R. Sandoval
Santa Fe, NM

Aunt Aga as La Llorona

Placita Rafaela is a cul-de-sac off the Acequia Madre in Santa Fe, and is a *barrio* where a branch of the Garcia family has lived for many generations.

Ageda Garcia, wife of Epifanio Garcia, was the matriarch of the whole clan – not just of her own children, but her grandchildren, great grandchildren, and all the other relatives who lived in that compound. She even had authority over the animals, of which she owned four or five dogs and at least three cats. Epifanio was a hardworking man who was employed for more than fifty years at the Boyle greenhouses, along with his son Alfonso, his nephews, and his grandnephews.

One evening, after Ageda (or "Tia Aga" as she was called by everyone) had worked hard all day, she went outside to call her son Alfonso and two of her nephews, Roberto and John, because it was their bedtime. After considerable hollering for the young boys to come into the house, she finally gave up trying. It was a beautiful spring evening and the aroma of the lilacs was everywhere – there was a feeling of summer in the air and many people were still outside.

Anyway, Tia Aga hit on the idea of climbing on some stilts and wrapping herself in a white sheet in an effort to convince the boys that she was *La Llorona* and that they had definitely better get into the house without fail! She figured that this method of threatening the little ones with an appearance by *La Llorona* would probably work, since nearly everyone was afraid of running into *La Llorona* because the compound was right off the acequia. And Tia Aga was that kind of person – she had a wonderful sense of humor and that is why everyone loved her so much. The fact that she cussed like a sailor didn't matter to anyone. She was the boss and commanded respect from the relatives as well as all of the neighbors.

Sneaking around the back of the house, she caught the boys by surprise. It was dark already, and all they could see was this terrifying creature, about seven or eight feet tall, coming toward them in a white shroud. As soon as she realized she had their attention, she started to whimper and wail in the same voice that everyone had heard from the real *La Llorona* at one time or another. She knew it was a very convincing performance, because she heard them gasp with fear and surprise and then scramble to get away from her. She felt gratified at her acting ability and thought to herself, "Good. I can use this every time these boys act up." But what happened was that John Martinez, a very mischievous boy who had been playing with the others, ran up to examine *La Llorona* and, in his enthusiasm, he tripped Tia Aga and knocked her off her stilts, and she fell flat on her bottom.

The Garcia family will long remember Tia Aga as *La Llorona!*

Margie Ulibarri
Santa Fe, NM

El Rancho de Los Maranos

People call me "Bushman" because I do landscaping for the movie companies. I'm the person who takes care of the vegetation, like trimming the shrubbery, etc. And I have a barbershop here in Albuquerque, so if I'm not cutting bushes, I'm cutting hair.

In 1943, when I was seven, I moved to East Grand Plains, New Mexico, a little farming community about twelve miles east of Roswell, to spend time with my Uncle Rumaldo, who practically raised me. The rest of my family was in Roswell opening up a business at the arcade there. One of the ranch-farms in East Grand Plains was named El Rancho de Los Maranos – "Pig Ranch" – which dates back to the early 1800s and sits on the path of the Chisholm Trail. Now it's called Oasis Ranch, which I guess they changed to make it sound a little better.

My uncle was a field foreman on this ranch and he would tell me that *La Llorona* traveled through the Hondo Valley into Roswell and then out to El Rancho de Los Maranos. This particular ranch had its own jailhouse, which they used in the earlier days, and its own company store. Sometimes there could be as many as a hundred and fifty people living at the *campo*, which is what they called the living quarters. *La Llorona* was supposed to have appeared on several occasions at the south end of the ranch in an area full of big cottonwood trees – what we call *alamos* – where the irrigation ditches were. When there was such a sighting, word would spread quickly throughout the *campo*. She'd float among the trees at dusk wearing a white cloak, moaning and screaming and scaring everybody half out of their minds. Since I worked on this ranch off and on for a number of years, I naturally became a real believer in *La Llorona*. It was impossible not to believe in her because of all the people who said they had seen her.

When I was eleven, I had to move from the ranch to East Los Angeles. During that time, I met all kinds of people from New Mexico, and all of them were very well acquainted with *La Llorona* – they had seen her in places like Deming and Silver City and a lot of the other smaller towns down in the southern part of the state. At that age, I believed she was a native of New Mexico. It never occurred to me that she might pop up somewhere else. So you can imagine how surprised I was to learn that she made regular appearances in a place called Coyote Pass in East L.A. There had been a gang killing there and the place had a real bad reputation that dated back many years. You could take your family there for a picnic during the day, but at night Coyote Pass was transformed into a dangerous jungle of sinful activity where the kidnapped, robbed, and murdered were dumped under the cover of night.

When I was fifteen, I moved back to El Rancho de Los Maranos and was put in charge of irrigating the ranch at the south end, which you may recall is the exact spot where *La Llorona* made her appearances. My uncle also told me that I was to do this work at night! Word spread very fast throughout the *campo* and soon my best friend Santos was making jokes that I should take a crucifix and flash it in her face if she appeared. Santos wasn't afraid of anything – in fact, his dad had been in Pancho Villa's army. I was more excited than scared, if you want to know the truth.

As it turned out, it was one of the roughest nights I had ever experienced as an irrigator. The ditch busted three times, the planted cotton broke up all night long, and the fields were getting so much water that the cotton that had grown out was pretty much destroyed. I spent the whole night shoveling

La Llorona

in a high wind and trying to secure the ditch caps, and I forgot all about *La Llorona.* I guess I thought to myself, "Only a fool would come out on a night like this."

At six o'clock the next morning, my uncle showed up with my replacement and the first thing he said when he got down from his pickup was, "Well, did you see her?" I said to him, "No, just a lot of wind." Later on, though, I thought to myself that maybe she had appeared by one of the trees and watched me work through the night. Could it have been *La Llorona* who made it such a difficult night for me?

Isidro Guerrero
Albuquerque, NM

The Sheepherder
Takes a Bath

My dad used to tell us this story that his grandfather had told him about one of the uncles in our family.

My family lived in Roy, New Mexico, where we used to have sheep that grazed in Ocate. During the time that the *gringos* were having their Civil War, about 1865, this brother of my great grandfather, Ramon Sanchez, never liked to take a bath from the time he had been a little *niño*. And he was always told that one of these days *La Llorona* was going to grab him and give him a good scrubbing. Ramon loved to be out there with his sheep in Ocate while they grazed. One day, one of the great grandmas went to the great grandpa, Juan José, who was the sheep owner, and told him, "You have to force Ramon to take a bath because we just can't stand the way he smells anymore. We have to sit and eat close to him and sometimes we have to chase him away so we can finish our food."

The *patron* went to talk to Ramon and they had a few words. That evening, they saw Ramon gathering wood and warming water near a hidden cove in the arroyo, around where the sheep grazed. Some of the family went to spy on him to see if he would really take a bath, and they watched him fill this wooden *cajete* with hot water and then get in. After a while, they got tired of watching him and went in to finish their chores.

Later, they all went outside because it was a warm evening and the moon was out. A long time passed until someone said, "Where is Ramon? It has been a very long time now since he went to take his bath." A couple of the old-timers decided to investigate and they went down to the arroyo and there he was, still sitting in the tub, scrubbing and scrubbing. One of them, Emilio, said to him, "Ramon, do you realize you've been in here half the night? Everyone is getting ready to go to sleep." Well, Ramon looked like he had seen a ghost. He kept scrubbing and scrubbing and he said to Emilio, "A woman came here and sat down right here, next to the *cajete,* and she told me that she would scrub the hide off my back if I didn't take a bath every week." Well, they had to force him to get out of there. He was wrinkled up like a raisin.

Later on, they said it was *La Llorona* who visited Ramon that night, because she was dressed in black, very beautiful, quite young, and she whimpered in this very low cry when she talked. The important thing, though, is that Ramon took a bath every week from that day on until he died of old age about sixty-five years later.

Irene Ortiz
Santa Fe, NM

The Courtyard Fantasy

I come from the Tates who founded the village of Taterville, near San Jose and San Juan in San Miguel County, New Mexico. I come from a family of artists. You might have known my late brother, Bill, who had a gallery on Canyon Road in Santa Fe for many years. I like to write books, myself.

I designed and built Emilio's restaurant here in Española. The chile they serve is out of this world, no question about it. If you've never been inside, it has a real authentic "Wild West" motif, with swinging doors like in a saloon and little booths that look like the inside of a stagecoach. People think those are real bullet holes in the walls, but the truth of the matter is, I ended up getting out my drill, turning it on, and running full speed ahead into the walls with the thing going full blast. I'd had a few beers and it seemed like a good idea at the time.

I ran away from home back in Tulsa when I was fourteen and rode just about every railroad line in this country and visited every state by the time I was twenty. I figure I traveled close to a quarter of a million miles either by freight or by thumb. I've got a lot of stories to tell as a result of my travels, but one of my favorites is that of the infamous and horrible *La Llorona,* the weeping woman, who strikes terror into the hearts of the innocent and leaves the guilty quivering in fear for their very souls.

Legend has it that this ghost woman we know as *La Llorona* travels at night from place to place, sometimes on a white horse and sometimes on a black horse. She is torn between good and bad – in other words, between Satan the Devil and God. Her soul or spirit is never at rest. She cries out at night in a sound of complete terror to please help her put her soul to rest.

Many of the New Mexico old-timers claim, in fact, that they have seen her setting on her horse in very remote places in northern New Mexico, mainly around rivers, streams, creeks and even dry arroyos, in her white robe, swinging a sword or whip and screeching very loud in a blood-curdling sound for you to follow her and she would lead you from the Devil and back to the Church. This was the good side of her spirit. On the bad side, she might curse and ask you to follow her to Hell, where she felt her soul might be resting. In short, her soul was lost and she was seeking same – it was in Heaven or Hell.

Many people say she did scare a heck of a lot of folks back into going to church and scared the little kids into being good.

I have a friend named Dennis who was born in Dixon, New Mexico. He is now fifty-five years of age, and he will swear he saw *La Llorona* when he was about nine or ten years old. His house was in a courtyard completely surrounded by an eight-foot wall with a gate at one end. One day, someone forgot to put the chain around the post to lock the gate, and in she came, into the courtyard on her white stallion, and then stopped at his house, where he and his two brothers and sister were playing marbles on the flagstone in the front. She never made a sound – just stood there for a couple of minutes. Then she rode away very fast, out the gate and into the dark.

Dennis said it scared them so bad that they never went out of the house for two days, and boy, were they good little boys and girls!!

George O. Tate
Española, NM

Mourning at Rosario Cemetery

On an early evening in 1943, I was playing on Jimenez Street near the Arroyo Mascaras here in Santa Fe with my friend Mary Alice Moya. It was around seven-thirty or eight o'clock when Mary Alice said to me, "Look over to the other side of the arroyo." I looked over there and I saw an old woman dressed in black with a *tapalo* – a shawl – over her head. Every three or four steps she took, she would raise her head and cry very low. Then she would lower her head like she was praying, and take another few steps.

She was heading toward the Rosario Cemetery from where the DeVargas Mall is now. My aunt Josefita Martinez, who is eighty-six, and my uncle Luis Martinez, who is eighty-four, said they used to see an old woman walking late in the evenings toward the Rosario Cemetery where the Rosario Chapel is.

A lot of people would say it was *La Llorona* checking on the people who had died. They would only see her when someone had just been buried.

Irene Ortiz
Santa Fe, NM

Great Balls of Fire

A section of what used to be the Old Santa Fe Trail was changed to College Street during the days of St. Michael's College. *Los Corchos de La Calle de El Colegio* – the "Corks" from College Street – used to talk about *las pelotas de lumbre y La Llorona* – the balls of fire and *La Llorona*.

The Corks were a gang of guys from Santa Fe who used to hang around together in the 1940s. They got that name because they drank wine. Wine bottles in those days didn't have screw tops like some of them do now.

One of the *Corchos*, Dickie Archuleta, was going towards La Calle Tenorio through College Street when he met up with Salvador Tucker. Salvie was coming from downtown and had taken a shortcut through East DeVargas Street and cut across the old *camposanto* – the cemetery grounds – which is the present location of the PERA Building where many state workers are employed.

I understand that when the local politicians decided to build the PERA Building on Catholic cemetery property, they unceremoniously dug up the bodies and, in cahoots with certain church officials, buried them somewhere else. There are a lot of people still living today that had family members dug up this way. When you think about it, it was a terrible thing to do to the families of these poor people, if that is what really happened.

People say that *La Llorona* turns the lights on and off in the PERA Building to this day. In fact, many of the office workers have seen her in broad daylight, and the cleaning crews hear her slamming doors and crying in the night. When she is seen, she is usually walking down one of the hallways, all in black, and as she walks, she slowly fades into nothing. Other times, people can hear her feet on the back stairs, but she is invisible. She has even thrown someone down the stairs, but that's another story.

Anyway, to get back to the *Corchos,* Dickie claims to this day that after he and Salvie crossed the *camposanto* and then headed down Manhattan and up College Street, *La Llorona* was right behind them throwing big falls of fire up the street toward Camino de Las Animas, which as you may already know, means "Street of the Spirits."

Demetrio Lujan
Pueblo, CO

La Llorona Haunts Arroyo Seco

I'm an artist and have lived in Taos, New Mexico all my life. My ancestry is a mixture of Apache and Spanish, and I'm a proud U.S. Army veteran, honored to have served this great country. I'd like to relate a horrifying incident that occurred many years ago north of Taos, in Arroyo Seco, to the Casias brothers. I was an eyewitness to this because they shared their experience with me minutes after it happened, and I knew they were being truthful because of the stone-cold raw fear in their eyes as they told me about it.

On the day of the incident, the two brothers, who were seventeen and nineteen, had been up on the game trail, an area where people like to go to hunt and fish, to check for elk and deer tracks. Around the same time, I was walking up the game trail when I spotted the boys coming in my direction. They were running down the trail toward me in a kind of panicky way, and as they tried to run past me I grabbed one of them by the arm and asked what was going on. I thought maybe they had seen a bear, because it was bear season and one had been spotted the week before. Bobby Casias told me that while they were walking up the trail, they heard a soft sobbing that increased in volume as they approached, and then they saw a lady dressed completely in black, on her knees facing the remnants of an old brick wall. She was weeping and making motions like she was scratching or clawing at the wall, and they noticed her dress was tattered and that the skin on her arms looked white and scaly, like a fish belly.

The boys, being raised to be respectful, asked her if she was okay. She stopped her scratching and looked at them, and they saw that she was a young woman with big brown eyes and her mouth was open and turned down. Then she turned back and continued clawing at the old wall, but her crying gradually turned into a very loud wailing, truly horrible. When they asked her again if she was all right, she turned her head and looked at them for a second time, and what they saw was something completely different – a decayed face with empty sockets where her eyes once were. As the boys stood frozen with shock, she slowly rose to her feet and started toward them, her arms outstretched and her fish-scale hands opening and closing as if to grab them. That was enough for them, and they turned and ran as though death was snapping at their heels. Later, Bobby said that when they told their mother what happened, she said that was *La Llorona* coming to claim her lost children, and the three of them fell to their knees and prayed the rosary for a good half hour.

A year or so later, my buddies and I and the Casias brothers went up the game trail to where the wall was, but everything looked pretty much the same except that there was a very odd feeling in the air, and we all thought it prudent to get out of there as quickly as we could. To be honest with you, I didn't go back up there for a long time after that.

John "Dark Wolf" Bucklin
El Prado, NM

Los Tecolotes En El Techo

I was born in 1909 in Mora, New Mexico. Back then it was the New Mexico Territory. I live by the church in the area they now call China, by some *acequias*. I lived in Santa Fe for a while in the 1930s.

My father used to tell me *La Llorona* dressed like a witch. When I was very small, we owned a house that is now called St. Joseph Hall, where they have meetings. Owls used to gather on the roof, sometimes ten at a time. My dad used to say they were witches. When they came down from the roof, they turned into women dressed in black. You couldn't see their faces. The leader was dressed in white and she was said to be *La Llorona*.

If you called the name "Jesus Christ," or like the *viejitos* – the old people – used to say, *"Jesus, Maria y José,"* or if you cried out, "Oh, my God," they would jump back and fly up and then vanish in thin air. Isn't that something? It was very frightening to us.

We moved to California after that and sold the house. When we came back, we lived in a house behind the meeting hall. The people who bought our old house were hardly ever there. My dad said something must have

La Llorona

scared them off.

We don't see the owls anymore. It's different, now. And the children only believe what they see on TV.

Margarita Olivas
Mora, NM

Ramon Garcia's Last Date

Around 1925, this man, Ramon Garcia, used to go out with different women. His wife wasn't the jealous type, but she was very religious and she didn't want him to be stepping out and all that jazz, you know? She said to him one time, "If you go out tonight, something's going to happen to you. You're going to meet up with the wrong party." He thought to himself, "She doesn't know what she's talking about."

So he went down to this bar called *La Rendija* – "The Crack" – and he had a couple of drinks. He danced for a while and it got to be about two in the morning, so he started walking home. Right where Canyon Road meets Garcia Street, he spotted this woman walking in front of him. She looked very attractive, very enticing. He was maybe twenty or thirty feet behind her, so he decided to walk a little faster.

When he finally caught up to her, he saw that she was wearing a heavy veil over her face. So he lifted the veil to see her better, and to maybe give her a kiss, and as soon as he did that, he realized that he was looking right into the face of *La Llorona*. With the rays of the moon shining on her face, she looked like a skeleton.

Ramon Garcia never stepped out on his wife again. He died not too long ago, and he said that he would never forget this experience.

Fred Montoya
Santa Fe, NM

Brownie

I grew up in Fort Garland, Colorado, which is in the San Luis Valley and the very heart of La Llorona country. My dad worked as a hand at Trinchera Ranch, which back in the 1950s and 1960s was a working ranch with thousands of head of cattle and sheep herds. Part of my father's job was driving the general manager's eight-passenger 1949 green Chevy suburban to pick up the hired hands for a day's work. The other part of his job was managing the summer cabins that were on our property and were rented out to vacationers. My grandma, who owned the cabins, lived next door to us. She was a wonderful person who had a strong influence on me, and I spent more time with her than I did with my own family.

Norfe was an elderly Irishman who lived in one of the cabins with his Newfoundland Brownie, a beautiful dog with white markings on his chest and paws. As the summer came to an end, Norfe told me he couldn't keep Brownie and asked me if I would like to have him. I had fallen in love with this huge beast, who was gentle and loving, and so I accepted without hesitation. The problem was that my dad saw dogs as generally useless if they weren't working dogs, and although Newfoundlands are working dogs, they have to be trained first. Brownie didn't know anything about herding sheep; he only knew how to slobber all over the kids who used to gather around and hug him. Although I managed to talk my father into letting us keep Brownie, he didn't really like Brownie and pretty much ignored him. So my grandma and I basically took care of him, grooming him and feeding him and giving him lots of love and attention. But the more my dad didn't want Brownie, the more Brownie loved my dad.

A few months after we got Brownie, when I was ten, something happened that changed my father's attitude toward Brownie for the rest of that dog's life.

One morning at sunrise, my father was getting ready to pick up the hired hands and drive them to work at Trinchera Ranch. As he walked down the road to the Chevy suburban, Brownie got up from the front yard and ran after him, and began growling and showing his teeth when they got to the bus. Right then, my father realized that Brownie was barking at a silhouette sitting in the driver's seat. He watched in horror as the silhouette drifted through the open door of the bus wearing a long black lacy dress, and then slowly glided up into the sky in the brisk, cold wind. Truth be told, my dad had a bit of a hangover that morning from too much celebrating the night before, and so you might question his credibility, except that Brownie had stopped growling at that point. Anyway, my father regained his composure and went on to pick up the hired hands. When all the workers were on the bus, he told them how Brownie had scared *La Llorona* away. The workers laughed and harassed him for the rest of the day, attributing his story to hallucinations from all that drinking the night before.

There is good news and bad news. First, my father acquired a new respect for Brownie, so that's the good news. The bad news is that I was second best to Brownie more than ever, because Brownie then became my dad's dog. Back then I believed it was all *La Llorona's* fault, but Brownie went on to live a long and happy life getting attention from the person he loved the most.

Lydia Ortiz Avant
Fort Garland, CO

The Road From Puerto De Luna

This is a story about a terrible experience I had with *La Llorona* and how it changed my life for the better.

About four years ago on the Fourth of July, I decided to walk the road from Puerta de Luna to the Nuestra Señora del Refugio Church in Santa Rosa, which I think is about six miles – maybe more. This is the same area, by the way, where there was a big shootout with Billy the Kid once. In fact, there are bullet holes in one of the buildings there. Anyway, the church was having its centennial and there had been celebrations going on for most of the day. Unfortunately, I got started late, but I decided to try and make it anyway before it got too dark out. Little did I know that something would happen to me on the road that would make me get there faster than I ever thought was possible.

I had gone about two miles and I was saying my rosary as I walked along, trying to say it with a feeling of sincerity because I was doing penance, and also trying to hurry a little bit because it was already starting to get dark. I was approaching this little bridge where the road turns very sharply to the right, when I heard what I thought was a wolf howling from the bosque, a little patch of woods, off to the right and up ahead of me. It was a very sad kind of howling, very drawn out but real loud, but as it faded it began to sound more like the cry of a woman. At that moment, I knew I was hearing the sound of *La Llorona,* because this was the same area of the river where others had heard her. As I tell this story, I feel the same fear I felt then. I can't describe to you how terrifying this was because there was no one around – everyone was at the church and the few houses I had passed along the road were dark and deserted.

Right then and there, I began to say my rosary as loudly as I could: "Holy Mary, Mother of God, pray for us sinners now and at the hour of our death, amen." And I said it louder and louder as I approached the bridge that went over the little river that separated me from the bosque and *La Llorona.* As I moved toward the bridge, I could feel the sweat pouring off of me. My heart was pounding and my legs felt shaky and weak as I pictured her suddenly stepping out and confronting me in the road. I knew that I still had a long way to go and that there was no turning back. It was like this was a test for me.

After I finally got across the little bridge, I ran all the rest of the way, hollering the rosary as loud as I could to try to drown out the sound of the howling that seemed to be right behind me. When I got to the church, I fell to my knees and realized I had reached the last bead. At that moment, I understood that my faith was stronger than ever, and it still is. I know that will never change. So for that reason, I feel that God put *La Llorona* in my path to strength my belief in Him.

Ernest Lucero
Albuquerque, NM

El Borracho on the Santa Fe River

They call me *El Enano* – The Dwarf – and I am sixty-four years old, now. I have lived in Santa Fe all my life except when I was in World War II – the Big One.

My dad used to talk about an incident that occurred when *El Gallina*, Manuel Montoya, was Chief of Police in Santa Fe in the 1940s. He was a good man. He would buy groceries for the poor out of his own pocket during Christmas, and he would provide a "little hair of the dog" to *los borrachos* – the winos – when they had hangovers. Everybody liked and respected *El Gallina*.

There was a *borracho* who lived on Lopez Street and his name was Juan de Dios Lopez. I use this name and not his real one so as not to insult his *familia*. One night, the Chief was driving a police car on Alto Street near Closson Street and some people ran to him as he was driving by and said that someone was drowning in the Santa Fe River. So *El Gallina* got out and looked, and there was Juan de Dios Lopez struggling in the water crying for assistance. These other people, I guess they couldn't swim. So *El Gallina* jumped into the river and saved this poor soul who was crying for his life.

Juan had been beat up and his nose was bleeding very bad. He was white as a sheet, ready to pass out. The Chief took him home and Juan told him that *La Llorona* had beat him up! And that she said to him, *Si te vuelvo a ver pedo, te vuelvo a golpear* – If I see you drunk again, I will beat you up again."

This happened to Juan when was about twenty-five years old, and I know he lived to be at least a hundred, so he had seventy-five years of being sober because after *La Llorona* beat him up that night, he never had another drink. And with the money he saved from not drinking, he built his family a very fine home on Calle Lopez.

El Enano
Santa Fe, NM

The Tiny Screamer

There was a real short guy, no more than maybe five feet or five feet one, by the name of Padilla. He was the *mayordomo* of the Acequia Madre in Santa Fe, the "mother ditch" that flows into the Santa Fe River. The *mayordomo* is the person who is assigned to supervise the maintenance of the *acequias* by the residents of a given neighborhood or *barrio*. In the older days, this assignment assured that everyone would have irrigation water for their gardens, that it flowed nicely, and there was no debris in it. The *mayordomo* is still a prestigious and important position in all the villages of northern New Mexico and it is a great honor to be given the title. I understand that the federal government has put aside millions of dollars for these villages to use to work on their *acequias,* as a matter of fact.

Anyway, to get back to the story, this guy Padilla was always down at the Acequia Madre. He took his job very seriously. He spent all of his time clearing the weeds and rocks that the kids used to throw in there in those days. Back in the old days, you didn't have beer cans, soda cans, candy wrappers, all this junk that people throw on the ground now. People used to save any liquor bottles or other bottles they had. They always could find another use for them. In fact, no one threw anything away in those days.

One evening, Padilla was around San Antonio Street and Acequia Madre. This was in the late spring and there were weeds everywhere, and he had been pulling them for quite some time and had made a little pile of them in the road that he planned to burn later. Something made him look up, and there was this little tiny boy standing across the road, and the kid was crying up a storm, weeping and wailing and just creating a real racket. Now, Padilla was a nice guy and he had kids of his own, and his heart just about melted seeing this tiny little kid in some kind of trouble, so he started across the road to get a better look at the boy and to find out who he belonged to. As he started toward him, though, the kid started screaming even louder. And the louder he screamed, the taller he seemed to grow, So by the time Padilla got to him, the kid was as tall as Padilla and still growing, and his screaming was deafening. Padilla dropped his rake and ran like hell with his hands over his ears. He turned around at one point, just to take a peek while he was running, and you're gonna say I'm lying, but the kid was probably a good nine feet tall and still growing.

From that day forward, Padilla told everyone that he had seen *La Llorona's* son. He said the way the kid grew so fast was a perfect example of an old Spanish saying: *"Tanto hace el Diablo con su hijo hasta que lo mata* – The devil does so much with his son until he kills him" – and that is the way the story is told to this day by the old timers in that neighborhood.

Alfonso "Trompo" Trujillo
Santa Fe, NM

88

La Llorona

The Rabbit Coat

In Villanueva, New Mexico, in the area south of the river by the old arroyo, was a place where the villagers used to dump their trash. While it was a well-known fact that *La Llorona* haunted arroyos, she was also frequently seen in various dump areas. The people used to say that they would see her at this particular dump area on Saturdays – never any other day.

In 1918, when I was still a little girl, my grandmother, Maria Isabel, told me that my grandfather, Juan Del Rio, took his .22 rifle out one morning to hunt for rabbit, and when he returned the next day, he told her that he had shared fried rabbit with a very strange woman dressed in black who kept whimpering and looking around as though she had lost something. He had never seen this lady in any of the surrounding villages or ranches, and he knew everyone for miles around.

It seems that he had gone out to the dump area on this particular Saturday and had shot a rabbit near the arroyo. This was a good place, of course, for finding rabbit because they would look for food there. He was roasting it and cleaning the *cuero* – the skin – when this lady appeared out of nowhere and asked if he would share the rabbit with her because she was very hungry and tired from looking for her little boy and little girl. My grandpa was a very kindhearted person, very generous and very sociable. He gave her his *zalea* – sheepskin – that he kept rolled up on his horse for warmth because she was shivering, and he told her to make herself comfortable by the fire.

While they were eating the rabbit, she very sadly told my grandpa that her children had wandered off to play when their wagon train had stopped to water the horses. Knowing that no wagon train had come through that area for many years, my grandpa asked her exactly when that had happened, and she replied, "Oh, about the time we first came here from the south, maybe 100 or 150 years ago." Then she told him she was going to her cave and would return with a gift for his wife, and she disappeared. He got up and looked around trying to see what happened to the *cuero del conejo,* the rabbit skin, and realized that she had taken it with her but had left the *zalea* behind.

Grandma Isabel said that a week later they got up to go to the church and found a beautiful rabbit skin coat by the front door with a note written in a very beautiful and educated script that said, "Juan Del Rio, you are a good man to strangers and this gift for your wife is from a lady that wanders the earth looking for the good in man and her lost children."

My grandmother wore that coat for many years and it never showed any signs of wear.

Maclovia Guerin
Denver, CO

Terrorizing Las Colonias

I would like to tell of an incident that happened to a group of people many years ago. At that time I was fifteen, and my husband Alfonso, my brother-in-law José, and my cousin Isidro had traveled from Las Vegas, New Mexico to Avondale, Colorado, near Pueblo, to work in the fields. There were some houses that were loaned to the workers there. The house we stayed in was a very long one, and there were three or four families staying in it.

Around twelve-thirty one morning, we heard a loud noise, a terrible wailing sound, coming from the river about a half-mile away. It woke everyone up, not just in our house, but also in all of the surrounding houses. Everyone ran outside and the cry was as loud as could be and it seemed very close. All of us knew right away it was *La Llorona*.

Alfonso and some other men decided to get in the car and investigate. The car had spotlights – the kind people used back then to blind the deer. The ones who stayed behind could see them with the spotlight when they got to the river.

The crying continued. It was so loud that it made our ears ring. Well, what happened was that they heard the cry coming from the other side of the river, so they drove around to get to the other side through a shallow area in the water, and as soon as they got there, the sound of the crying would then seem to be coming from the opposite side. So they would have to cross the river again. This happened about four times, maybe more. Then it stopped as suddenly as it started.

We lived there in the *colonias* – the settlement – for three months. There was a *capilla* – a little chapel – on the property, but they never held Mass. See, these *colonias* were away from the town; they were for people working in the fields, and there wasn't a priest available to travel that far. There was a cemetery next to the *capilla*, and on the night *La Llorona* came to the river, there was an unusual sound that seemed to come from inside like the buzzing of bees, but very loud. It was very strange and scary. The buzzing lasted almost a half hour, and then it all stopped.

The next day, we went to the *capilla* to see if there was anything unusual there, but there was no sign of anything.

Joann Baca
Santa Fe, NM

The Man who Wouldn't go to Church

There was this *vato* – this guy – who never wanted to go to church. His wife always wanted to have her husband be an example to their children, but he didn't care. He liked to sleep late on Sundays, sit around and eat doughnuts and drink coffee, read the paper, and so on. He said church services got in the way of these important activities. Besides, he told his wife, "God already knows what I believe, so who do I have to prove it to?" She left it at that. She would get the three kids up early for Sunday Mass and have them dressed and out the door by five-thirty a.m. for the walk to church. Most of the time, they'd be back before he was even out of bed.

On Saturday morning during Lent, though, his wife said to him that he should at least think of her and the kids and just this once he should go with them to mass. Instead of being a nice guy about it, what does he do? He gets mad and goes out and gets drunk!

While he was heading home, about three or four in the morning, *La Llorona* stopped him and lectured him about his not being a good father, about how he should go to church, etc. etc. He told *La Llorona* to mind her own business! Well, that was all she needed to hear. So she took him and tied him to the door of the church, and that's where they found him the next morning. He was very mad. While his friends were untying him, he was bragging in a loud voice that *La Llorona* wasn't going to force him to do anything – he was a real stubborn guy.

But as stubborn as he was, it seems like the village residents found this guy tied to the church doors every Sunday morning. Sometimes he'd have a black eye, or his clothes would be torn. He was always a mess.

After about six months he'd finally had enough. I guess he just got tired of it. So he ended up making a deal with *La Llorona*. If she didn't bother the *borrachos* – the winos – in the neighborhood, and as long as they bothered no one else, he would see to it that all of the neighborhood *borrachos,* himself included, would go to church every Sunday. What happened was that most of these *borrachos* quit drinking and straightened out their lives.

So that's how a miracle occurred in that particular neighborhood.

Ruben Chavez
Santa Fe, NM

El Dia De San Geronimo y La Noche De La Llorona

This story was told to me by a fellow who died about twenty years ago, when he was seventy-eight. I will not mention his name because his widow is still alive and so are his six children and many grandchildren.

In the early 1920s, this fellow had a white horse that he used to ride around, a real nice looking horse. One night, there was a big dance in the village of Agua Fria to celebrate the Festival of San Geronimo. Well, this fellow's father told him not to go to the dance and especially not to take that particular horse, since it would get tired. See, the horse had been worked heavily that day in the fields and the village was a good five or six miles down the road. Just to make sure that his son wouldn't go, the father said to him, "I'll put a curse on you. If you go out, something bad will happen to you." The guy said to himself, "My dad's old-fashioned. An old timer."

And so off he went on the white horse, which was called Blanco. About midnight, he decided to start home from the dance. He would have stayed longer, but it was getting cloudy and there was only a half moon. Across from the Santa Fe River on Alameda Street, he spotted something moving around on the ground right near the front of his dad's house. He couldn't see too good because it was dark, first of all, and second of all, this thing was in the rabbit bushes. That's what we call the *chamiso* because the rabbits used to hide in it when we hunted them.

So he got off Blanco and walked over to this thing, which looked in the dark like an animal of some kind. It was just lying there and not moving, and when he reached down and touched it, he could feel clothing. So he figured then that it was a person. He realized that it was lying face down, so he rolled it over and then he could see that it was a woman, about four feet tall. At that exact moment, the half moon came out from under a cloud and he saw that this thing had a beak, like a bird, and then it started wailing. He recognized the sound right away because he had heard *La Llorona* at night by the river, and now here he was looking right into her terrible face.

He let go of this thing and ran into the house. He told his dad about it and his dad said to him, "So the curse came true."

Fred Montoya
Santa Fe, NM

Eduardo

On that cold fall evening when he first heard *La Llorona*, Eduardo had just finished sweeping the long marble hallway in the PERA Building and had met his wife downstairs at the main doors to pick up the dinner she had prepared. She kissed him and reminded him to bring home the dishes at the end of his shift; he always seemed to forget. He returned inside the building, past the high, fresco-covered walls, down the stairwell to his niche. There, on his stool in front of the heater, he unwrapped the fresh-roasted chile, still-warm tortillas and the little foil package of *chicharrones,* and poured another cup of hot coffee. He leaned down toward the electric heater at his boot and heard someone clearly say, "*Darkness.*" The red glow from his heater faded, and the power blew inside the PERA Building.

But it hadn't. Five seconds later, power restored, Eduardo sat back on his stool, the voice hanging over him like a cliff. *Darkness.* A sharp voice. A woman's voice. Then, a swift movement passed by his janitor's room. Eduardo leaped into the hall, his flashlight bouncing over the high walls, catching sight of a woman with long black hair, clutching a black shawl to her face as if

La Llorona

frightened. A low whimper came from behind her dark robe. Eduardo saw her fade to black as the power shut down once more.

The cold air outside the PERA Building hit Eduardo in the face as he ran out the front doors. He stopped when he reached the street and turned around, but the lights were all on again and everything looked the way it should look. At that moment, Eduardo reached into his memories for the *La Llorona* stories the *viejitos* used to tell on the Santa Fe Plaza. He always thought they were making them up.

The doors of the PERA Building swung open. Two glowing embers the size of snowballs shot out of the building and headed straight for Eduardo as he ran up the Santa Fe Trail. It was dawn when he returned to his home. His wife was just starting the fire. She wanted to know why he forgot his dinner dishes again.

Sam Welch
Beverly Hills, CA

La Llorona De La Junta

I was born in Missouri and lived for a time in La Junta, Colorado, a small town of about 8,000 people. There were nine kids in my family, four older than me, and four younger. La Junta is basically desert, but the land is used for raising cattle.

We were a close-knit family – a clan, really – and I took care of my two younger sisters, but I hung around with my two younger brothers every chance I got. I was a tomboy and we pretty much ran wild. We used to take long hikes in the summer through fields full of rattlesnake – sometimes you'd see twenty or thirty of them either basking in the sun or lying asleep under rocks. Occasionally, I could hear them rattle but I was never afraid. We'd learned somewhere that if you were quiet and respectful, they'd never bother you. We also used to see lots of scorpions and tarantulas. It wasn't unusual for the temperature to get up to 120. One time, we fried some eggs on the sidewalk near our house and our mother caught us. She was very angry because eggs were a precious commodity for a family of nine kids.

In the 1960s, I was attending a Catholic school, and I guess I was about thirteen or fourteen when a bunch of us decided one summer night that it might be fun to go to the cemetery with candles and a Ouija board and call up some spirits. In retrospect, I can't believe we used to do that, because I personally think it's very dangerous. But we visited the cemetery every chance we got that summer.

We actually used to hear voices around the graves. My friends would say to me, "That's *La Llorona* coming to get you, Barbara, because you're blonde, and *La Llorona's* lost child is blonde, too. So if she comes here, she'll grab you and not any of us." I bought this ridiculous story and was really frightened by it, but for some reason I never ran out of there and went home. When we weren't using the Ouija board, we used to talk about *La Llorona*. She was an endlessly fascinating subject for us. We continued to do this calling up of the spirits for another summer before we decided that there were more interesting things to do, like go out with boys, for example.

Now and then we'd also go down to this area where there was an arroyo with a wooden bridge running across it. It ran in July of every year, and we'd stand around on the bridge and throw rocks into the water and talk about how *La Llorona* was looking for her two kids that had died somehow – I don't recall if any of us really knew how they had died – but the story was that if she found us she'd take our spirits. This particular bridge held a special attraction for us because we used to hear a terrible, eerie, plaintive wailing that seemed to travel from underneath the bridge and up the sides of the arroyo. I can't sufficiently describe to you how very much it actually sounded like a woman wailing. It was the wind, of course, and I'm sure a meteorologist or physicist would explain the dynamics of that to me now, but at the time we much preferred to believe that it was *La Llorona* we were hearing.

Strangely enough, I now live in an area of Santa Fe on the Acequia Madre where there have been many, many sightings of *La Llorona* over the years. Sometimes, when I am out walking my dog, I imagine that I can hear her wailing nearby. I am a weaver by profession and now I'm trying to incorporate my idea of her into some of my landscape tapestries. Now that I think of it, it seems amazing that *La Llorona* has been a part of my life in one way or another since I was in elementary school.

Barbara Berger
Santa Fe, NM

The Robe

As a young boy growing up in Belen, New Mexico back in the 1950s, I heard the story of *La Llorona* many times. There were several versions, but the one I used to hear the most often was from my grandma, who said that *La Llorona* had lost her two children and desperately needed to find them, and when she saw a child that looked like one of hers, she would start screaming in agony and then try to grab it. The reason she was always near the river was because that's where she had lost them, supposedly by drowning. My grandma also used to say that *La Llorona* had the ability to judge others because she lived in another world where the past, present, and future were one.

When I was around fourteen, a new kid, Billy, moved into the neighborhood, and we hit it off right away. I admired him because he wasn't afraid of anything, and I think he liked me because I fed his big ego. He chain-smoked, which I thought was very cool, and dismissed as "stupid" all of the things I had been taught to value at birth. Not only that, he talked about how he was going to drop out of school, get himself tattooed and join the navy when he turned sixteen. Billy was from the *barrios* of East Los Angeles and knew everything – a real sophisticated and mature kind of guy, I thought. Of course, my parents forbade me to associate with him, but Billy called me "chicken" for allowing my parents and grandparents to push me around. This was around the time of the Korean War and there was a lot of publicity in the newspapers about American soldiers being brainwashed by the Koreans. Billy warned me about losing my ability to even think for myself. I was putty in his hands.

So I began climbing out of my bedroom window late at night to meet Billy and his gang. There were a half dozen of them, and they had chains they would drag around in case they got into a "rumble" with a rival gang from another neighborhood – which never happened. Instead, they'd just stand around smoking cigarettes and throwing around four-letter words and discussing strategies for various illegal activities, like stealing auto parts. For a while I liked being part of this gang, but it began to get old real quick – to be honest with you, these guys weren't very bright. I hate to say it, but as the saying goes, the group as a whole was one taco short of a combination plate.

After a couple of weeks of this, I realized that these guys were probably going to end up in jail at some point, and probably so would I. I could just picture my mother and father coming to bail me out and what a living hell my life would be after that. So one hot night in August, I'd had enough, and I snuck back into the house with a new resolve – I would come up with some kind of excuse for not seeing Billy and his friends again.

As I lay back against the pillow, relieved that I had finally made this decision to straighten out my life, I happened to look down toward the end of my bed. Well, there she was, the light of the half moon showcasing her like a Renaissance painting in a museum – *La Llorona,* seated in my rocking chair, as motionless as a statue. I could see that she looked almost exactly as I had always pictured her, with the exception of a long braid that fell over her left shoulder. She wore her dark cloak securely wrapped around her with a hood that almost completely covered her pale, twisted, and ancient face. Her mouth lay slackly open as if prepared to emit a silent scream, and I could see tiny little fangs glistening in the dim moonlight. As I lay there frozen, waiting for whatever fate *La Llorona* had chosen for me, I wondered, fleetingly, why *La Llorona* was sitting in my bedroom and not Billy's. What had I ever done to deserve this?

And so I have come to the end of my story. As you can see, I am still here. Of course, it was not *La Llorona* sitting in my rocking chair that August night. It was my bathrobe, a dark brown corduroy thing thrown carelessly over the back of the chair, a robe that my mother had made on her Singer sewing machine. It was an unusual bathrobe because it had a gold braid that served as a tie around the waist, which used to be a pull for some old draperies from the living room. And it had a hood that I could wear over my head on those cold nights when it was necessary to make a trip to the outhouse.

Billy's family moved back to Los Angeles a few months later. Occasionally, I wonder whatever happened to him. I'm glad I knew him for that brief period, though. The best lessons are always learned early in life.

Robert Gonzales
Rio Rancho, NM

The Last Dance

On Labor Day in 1952, the last day of *Fiestas* in Santa Fe, one of my sisters passed away. I was twelve years old and part of a large family. While the members of my family grieved her loss, the rest of the city celebrated the most important and exciting weekend of the entire year. My father sent the younger children, including myself, out of the house and told us to keep busy doing other things while they made funeral arrangements and received visitors. My dad had one strict rule though: be home by midnight.

So I spent the day and evening wandering around and observing the various events. Everyone was dressed up in their *Fiesta* outfits – the ladies in full ruffled skirts and fancy blouses, wearing all their finest turquoise and silver, and the men in Mexican *charro* outfits or their best *torero* – bullfighter – costumes. The *villeros alegres* played their guitars or fiddles, while others danced in the streets or went to private parties. This was, and still is, a weekend when everyone, and I mean everyone, celebrates.

As the day – and then evening – wore on, I found myself in the area of the old Guadalupe Bridge, which was near where *El Baile,* the final dance of the *Fiesta* weekend, was taking place. Hundreds of people swirled around in the street in colorful costumes to music from *mariachis,* and the atmosphere was electric with excitement as many dancers mingled with people who were passing by and had stopped to watch. I found myself watching from the sidelines with several others who were too young or too shy to participate. While I was not really involved because of the sadness I was feeling at the time, I was still mesmerized by the magic of that evening.

There were other people besides myself who were passive participants, one of them an elderly woman of about eighty. I noticed her several times that evening, probably because no matter where I wandered, she always seemed to be a few feet away. It didn't seem unusual, though, since there were also several other people I kept seeing here and there.

At some point, I realized that it was almost midnight and that no matter how fast I ran home, I would never make it on time. But I decided to try anyway, and so I started doing a fast jog across the bridge and toward our house, which was a half-mile away on West Manhattan Street. As I trotted along, I began to realize that someone was behind me and keeping up with me no matter how fast I ran. When I hit the corner on Romero Street, I glanced back to see who it was and almost fell over when I realized it was the same old lady I had seen back at *El Baile.* At that point I really put some smoke behind me and practically fell when I stumbled to our back door, which was unfortunately locked. I banged and banged with my fists, but everyone was in front of the house and couldn't hear me, I guess. I was too scared to turn around and see if the old lady was approaching, but I imagined that she was practically on top of me. Finally, I ran around to the front and threw myself, completely out of breath, at the feet of my surprised family. I was never so glad to see a group of people in my life as I was at that moment. When I told my dad what had happened, he said to me, "It's all in your mind. It's because of your sister." But he went outside and looked around anyway, just to make sure.

There were a lot of *La Llorona* stories floating around in those days, and many of them revolved around the idea that if a person misbehaved, they'd run into *La Llorona.* But I'd done nothing wrong, and so I wonder to this day about that incident, even though no one can ever convince me it wasn't *La*

La Llorona

Llorona herself chasing me down that street.

Sometimes people would say to someone who had seen *La Llorona*, "You've had too much *mula*," which was the homemade whiskey the local people made out of corn or potatoes. I hardly need to tell you that the strongest thing I drank on that terrible night, at the tender age of twelve, was a Coke.

My dad used to make beer in our bathtub. No one could use the tub for the three or four days it would take to ferment. Then he'd put it in the bottles he'd collected. You never threw away bottles in those days because someone could always use them. Once in a while one of them would explode and it sounded like a gun going off. I remember seeing a kitchen cabinet door hanging by one hinge because a bottle on the shelf had blown up. God was looking out for us in those days because none of us ever got hit by flying glass.

You might ask why we didn't use kegs, which we could get at Theo Roybal's store. He sold the glass ones – I think they came from Mexico – but they were too small, really. Before that, folks used to use metal kegs and they'd poison the heck out of themselves because the beer interacted with the metal somehow and made people really sick.

Folks used to say, "On that stuff, you'd see anything." I guess that's true with the *borrachos*, anyway – all of them talk about *La Llorona!*

Herman Grace
Santa Fe, NM

107

Sister Cleo's Revelation

The Loretto Academy, a girl's school, used to be situated where the Inn at Loretto is now. Across the street was where Fred West, the very popular and well-respected justice of the peace, had his office. This street was, of course, the original Santa Fe Trail that went to La Fonda Hotel.

Sister Cleofitas was an old and beautiful nun who was perhaps no more than four and a half feet tall, and who would often walk up the Old Santa Fe Trail to the old *camposanto* – cemetery -- across from the Boyle greenhouse, where they specialized in carnations of all colors. Sister Cleofitas visited the *camposanto* often to place carnations on some of the graves and to keep the headstones clean. Each year, when the fruit blossoms appeared on the trees, she would spend many hours cleaning and weeding the areas around the graves with her rake and hoe. She was a kind, thoughtful, and generous person who truly loved God and her calling as a sister in her order, but the older she grew, the more she began to miss some of the nuns who had passed away before her, and who were now being replaced by young novices. Sometimes she would stand at the graves and talk to Sister Rosina and Sister Angelica, who lay side by side, and cry quietly into her little hands when she thought of the seemingly lonely years that lay ahead.

Late one hot summer afternoon, Sister Cleo was pulling some particularly stubborn weeds from around the headstone of Sister Miguela, and she was having a great deal of trouble pulling one weed that was nearly as tall as she was. As she struggled and puffed, she began to sense that she was not alone, and looked up to see a very tall woman in black standing over her. For a moment, Sister Cleo thought that the woman was another sister, but then realized that she was a stranger and wore a shawl over her had and had a pale and sad face. Sister Cleo squinted up at the lady, who asked her what she was doing. Sister Cleo, surprised, answered, "I am here to make certain that the flowers at the graves of the sisters are fresh and watered. It is only right to do so in honor of the dead."

The sad-faced woman said to Sister Cleo, "I cannot bury my children, for I cannot find them. They are lost in time and space, and it is my fate to search for them until the end of eternity. You have your friends right here, safe and protected. But they cannot smell the scent of these flowers. Take them to someone who can smell them." With these words, the woman faded away. Sister Cleo was naturally very startled by this encounter and shaken to her tiny little feet by these words of wisdom imparted to her.

Sister Cleo turned and began to walk toward the setting sun, leaving the hoe and the rake behind and the weeds in an untidy little pile. She walked past the unseeing eyes of Sister Angelica and Sister Rosina and Sister Miguela. She continued past the front gate, down the dirt road, and then turned west past the Loretto Academy. She moved more and more swiftly until her tiny little feet became a blur and she herself seemed to be carried by an unearthly wind.

It is said that Sister Cleofitas next appeared in India, ministering to the beggars and lepers. Many said that they had seen her that afternoon passing the Academy, and that she was young again and very beautiful like an angel.

Orlinda Tapia
San Antonio, TX

The Woman in White

I am eighty-four years old and live in El Llano de San Juan, a mountain village situated off the high road to Taos, east of Peñasco. It is very beautiful up here. In the old days, El Llano de San Juan was (and still is) a stronghold of the *Penitentes,* which is an offshoot of the early teachings of Catholicism. Some people say that after the Spaniards deserted the mountain villages in New Mexico, these people were left without religious leaders and so developed the *Penitente* beliefs and practices. Others say the tradition originated in Spain and was brought to this country by the Spanish *conquistadores.* Whatever the case may be, these *Penitentes* are humble people and their home is your home – *mi casa es su casa.* You are treated like royalty when you visit them.

I play the violin at *El Rancho de Las Golindrinas* in Santa Fe, a museum that recreates the style of living here that existed long ago when this part of the country was known as *Nueva España*, with weavers, religious observations, people cooking native dishes, and so on. There is a festival in October of each year that attracts thousands of people.

In 1930 or 1931, we were sitting by our house in El Turquillo. It was a

La Llorona

special occasion, and we had some of our sons there too. We had many cows in those days with a lot of pastureland. It was in the afternoon, and we were sitting by the house looking down the Lucero road, where there is a little creek that comes in from Guadalupita. We were gossiping and talking when all of a sudden, we saw a woman coming from that direction, all dressed in white. A very tall woman, at least nine feet. The whole family gathered in the yard to watch her. It gave me the chills.

She came down to the bottom of the ravine and started walking on the Lucero road, which goes by the front of our house, and when she got to the spot where she had to cross the river, she just seemed to float over the water. Then she started going up the hill and when she got to the top, she just disappeared in thin air. At a distance of about 500 yards, she reappeared. We watched her until she disappeared a second time.

Another time, we saw her doing the same thing. We could not tell if she wore shoes because her dress was very long – she might have been barefooted. We checked but found no tracks. People said then that she was *La Llorona*.

Patricio Lujan
Rodarte, NM

Ruben and Max

In May of 1943, Ruben and Max were employed as gravediggers at the San Jose Cemetery on Rincon Street in Las Vegas, New Mexico. This was a Catholic cemetery that also had the reputation of being *La Llorona's* hunting grounds. There had been many sightings of her in this area over the years, and few men wanted to take the job of gravedigger despite the fact that there was hardly any work to go around in those days.

Now, this was during World War II and people were nervous anyway because nearly everyone had a relative fighting overseas or knew someone who had been killed or wounded. It was not a time for *La Llorona* to be scaring people – there was already enough on their minds. But, since folks had the jitters from always thinking about death, now they talked about *La Llorona* more than ever. There were stories about her all over Las Vegas, and it seemed like a good many of these stories started on Saturday nights in the *cantinas* and then spread to the *barrios* from there.

Max and Ruben were digging a grave around this time in preparation for the burial of a Mr. Armijo, who would have been ninety-four years old had he been able to stay on this earth for just another week. As the saying goes, however, "*Pero cuando Dios te recuerda, te vas--* But when God remembers you, you're gone."

It was Good Friday, as a matter of fact, and the hour was growing late as the two men labored over the last *paladas de tierra* – shovels of dirt. They stopped for a few minutes to partake of some vintage wine that they had purchased a little earlier on their way to work. Ruben sniffed the cork to make sure it was the wine he was accustomed to drinking, and nodded in satisfaction – *gracias a Dios* that *vino de pata* could still be had for a decent price from the bootleggers. It was and always would be his favorite beverage.

As the two men rested against a cottonwood tree and shared the bottle of *vino de pata,* they looked up at the full moon as it began its ascent on the darkening horizon. At that moment, however, their peace was shattered by a terrible loud cry and the two startled men suddenly saw themselves looking straight at the figure of a woman in white striding toward them in the dusk. Max and Ruben, although they had never seen her before, instinctively knew that this was *La Llorona.* She quickened her approach toward them, her arms outstretched as if to grab them. At the same time, she let out a terrible, low wail that sounded like a wounded animal. Ruben and Max jumped to their feet and ran from the cemetery, never to return.

Now, every time Ruben and Max get drunk – which unfortunately is often – they talk about this experience with *La Llorona.* They have told this same story in every *cantina.* It is always the same but for one little detail: They say it happened on Bad Friday, not Good Friday.

Raymond Lovato
Las Vegas, NM

El Sanador

I was born in Chaparito, New Mexico in 1895. My father was a Presbyterian minister and my mother was a teacher.

My story is about a religious healer who came to the Mora Valley at the time of the great flood, which occurred in 1904. In the summer of that year, a *gringo* from Denver in a shiny and expensive suit arrived in town and moved into the rooming house across the road from us. Over the next few days, this city slicker told people that a very important person was coming to Mora, a man called *El Sanador* – "The Healer." Now, Mora was a quiet little town, so this generated a lot of excitement among the residents. I would sit by our front window every chance I got to watch for *El Sanador's* arrival. After a few days, the anticipation in town had built to such a fever pitch that there was always a little crowd of people standing across the street waiting for him.

On a Sunday afternoon about a week later, my parents and I were seated at the dinner table having a very fine meal of *carne adovada* and tortillas when we heard what sounded like a stampede coming down the main street. I ran to the window and there it was: A black buggy with four white horses, a driver, and *El Sanador* himself seated in the back wearing a white robe with a black shawl and sandals. He was a handsome young man with long black hair and a nicely trimmed beard. The driver jumped off the buggy and cleared a path for the crowd, and then the city slicker came running out of the house and unrolled a red carpet between the buggy and the doorway – I guess so *El Sanador's* feet would not touch the dirt. Then they assisted *El Sanador* down from the buggy and the three of them went inside the house. An hour later, there was a very long line of people outside.

The next day, I went over and peeked through the front window of the little rooming house. There was *El Sanador,* sitting in a big chair. People would kneel down before him and he would put his right hand on their head and say a prayer, and then I saw that his left hand was also stuck out with the palm up, to receive money! Having been raised by a Presbyterian minister, I knew that it was not customary for healers to accept money from people, especially the sick.

This activity went on for a week or so, with people starting to come in from the surrounding towns. Sometimes we couldn't sleep because of the racket. There were children playing, adults gossiping, dogs barking, even a vendor selling tamales and empanadas. My father went outside a few times to try to reason with people, but of course no one would listen because everyone had heard rumors about this person or that person receiving a miracle healing from *El Sanador.*

Then, a miracle occurred, what my father called an *intervención divina* – a divine intervention. It seems that there was a complaint registered with the authorities by the family of a Señor Jaramillo that after *El Sanador* had laid his hands on Señor Jaramillo's slightly arthritic knees, now his knees were worse than ever and he could only take a few steps before he would cry out in pain.

The day that the Jaramillo family registered their complaint, it was very sunny and warm, and the usual long line had formed in front of the rooming house. At the head of the line was a woman in a long black dress with a black veil. People said they could hear her whimpering, possibly from being in pain, but she did not respond to expressions of sympathy and kept her head down. After a few minutes, the door was opened to admit her, and as she stepped inside, the sky was suddenly filled with dark clouds and there was a loud thunderclap. Then the heavens opened up and it began to pour rain. As people ran for shelter under the trees nearby, they heard a terrible wailing from inside the house. Many of the witnesses said that the lightning and thunder from the storm was especially concentrated in the area of the rooming house, and my father said he could attest to that. It was a very frightening experience.

During this terrible night, the Sapello River between Mora and Las Vegas flooded and turned into a raging force that breached the banks and flooded homes all around. As the residents ran for their lives, they saw *El Sanador*, the city slicker, the driver, the horses and buggy, even the red carpet, being swept down the river, never to be seen again. What we did not know was that this was the beginning of the great flood of 1904, an historic event. Could *La Llorona* have been responsible for it?

Levi Madrid
Mora, NM

La Llorona goes to Middle School

My dad came to the U.S. from Monterrey, Mexico and worked as a gardener in California taking care of rich people's landscaping. He worked seven days a week and never took vacations. You will not find more hardworking people than the ones who come here from Mexico as young people and then work their way up over the years, and my dad was no exception. He met my mom in California and in a few years they had their own business, which they sold and then came to Tucson, where I was born. This was in the 1960s. My dad had developed bad arthritis by that time, probably from all those years as a gardener, and I remember he used to rub WD-40 into his joints every morning and every evening. He also would take a teaspoon of kerosene, the kind you light lamps with. He said it cured everything. He lived to be ninety-two, so maybe that's true, or maybe it was his good Mexican genes.

Our household was very traditional and before any of us kids went to the doctor, there were always the *remedios* that my mother would take down from the kitchen cabinet first. One time I was very sick with a terrible sore throat, so my mom made some hot chile caribe, which is a puree made from red chile pods. My dad took a big spoon of it and ordered me to swallow it. In those days you minded your parents on pain of death. It burned the hell out of my throat going down, but by the next morning my sore throat was completely gone. The other popular *remedio* was *oshá,* which is a root that heals just about anything. My dad used to keep a piece of it on a string that he hung around his neck. When he was under the weather, he would cut off a piece of it and make tea.

I loved going to school. I was always a good student, probably because my parents were very strict about homework. I had to get all of my homework done before I was allowed to do anything else. The middle school I went to was small compared to the other schools in Tucson. There were probably forty kids my age, half of them girls, and most of us were of Mexican descent and grew up with various superstitious beliefs. We rejected most of them, but the one belief that everyone hung onto was about the story of *La Llorona,* the weeping woman. Many of the girls insisted they had seen and heard her in one of the bathrooms, which meant that nearly everyone was afraid to go in there. My friend Erlinda said she had been washing her hands and looked up and saw a woman in a black veil float behind her going very slowly, and then she went right through the door and disappeared into the hallway. My other friend Barbara said she was in one of the bathroom stalls, and when she came out, *La Llorona* came out of the stall next to her and tried to grab her, which of course made her start screaming hysterically and then she passed out cold. Some kids thought maybe *La Llorona* had been a student at that school and was haunting the school because of some wrong that had been done to her by a teacher.

There were different names for *La Llorona* back then. Some people called her Mary Jane, Mary Wales or Bloody Mary, and if you stood in front of the mirror and said "*La Llorona, La Llorona,* you murdered your babies" twenty times, you could make her appear. Some of the braver girls would do this and then brag about how they weren't scared. I never tried it myself, needless to say.

It's forty years later and I still hear *La Llorona* stories here and there, and now she seems more popular than ever. I guess this is one legend that will probably never die. As long as there is Latino culture, there will be *La Llorona.*

Diana Martinez
Tucson, AZ

The Tragic Tale of La Llorona

I live in the Midwest now but I grew up in Texas, near Brownsville, where there are many *La Llorona* stories that have been brought here by people who came here from south of the border.

Here is the story I grew up with: *La Llorona* was a very beautiful young woman named Maria who grew up dirt poor in a Mexican village. One morning, her mother sent her to get water from the village well. As she was getting the water, a very handsome man on a white horse rode up to her and said, "I am very thirsty. Would you be so kind as to give me a drink of water from the well?" As soon as they looked into each other's eyes, they knew they were soul mates. Alas, they could not marry because he came from royalty and Maria was a humble poor girl, so he built a big house for her to live in and they had two children. He visited regularly for a while, but then his visits became less frequent until they stopped completely. Maria decided to visit the mansion where he lived, and walked for many hours until she reached the big front door. When she knocked, a servant came to the door and said he was not there because he had married a famous princess from Spain. Maria was

La Llorona

so angry that she went into a rage, and she went home and got her two kids and drowned them in the river and watched them float downstream. As soon as she gained her sanity moments later, she collapsed and died of grief on the riverbank. When she tried to enter Heaven, an angel stopped her and said she could not enter the afterlife until she found her children, and so she was forced back to Earth and condemned to wander the waterways of the world looking for her children forever. That is when she became the infamous and tragic *La Llorona.*

If you happen to be near water at night especially, you will hear *La Llorona* crying, *"Mis hijos, mis hijos* – my children, my children." Kids who grew up with this story were told to never go near a stream or river or creek or anything with water in it, because *La Llorona* would grab them and they would never be seen again. Even backyard swimming pools were problematic. The scary thing is that if her weeping sounds like she is nearby, that means she is far away, and if it sounds like she is far away, she could be practically on top of you, ready to grab you. People who have seen her actual face have never forgotten it – it is that horrible. From her centuries of crying, her skeletal face has red streaks that look like trails of blood, and her eyes are so hollow that if you look into them you can be permanently sucked in. Her mouth is just a terrible big hole with the sound of weeping coming from it day and night.

Marty Tenorio
South Bend, IN

La Llorona Escapes from the Police

I was listening to my shortwave radio one night, around 1984, and I had the
police frequency on. I don't know what time it was, but it was late, when I
heard this report that a lady in the El Torreon addition had called the police
because she said she could hear *La Llorona* crying down by the Santa Fe River.

There was a big rush to get over there—you wouldn't believe it! Five police
cars and three sheriff's cars. Well, I sat there for about a half hour listening to
the transmissions—it was really something. They'd hear crying by a tree and
they'd go over there, and there wouldn't be anything. Then they'd hear it from
somewhere else, and they'd all run over there, and of course there wouldn't
be anything there, either. They were saying it sounded like a baby crying. You
would have thought with all the transmitting back and forth that this was
Fiestas or some other big event.

Finally, one of them said over the radio, "We're never going to find her
because it's *La Llorona*." And that was the end of it. They all left.

La Llorona

Believe me, it happened—someone should go see if it's still in their records. I'll bet they erased it.

Cosme Garcia
Santa Fe, NM

La Monita

My grandmother, Ursula Chavez, told me that in the 1920s, two of her sons, who were my uncles, went to a dance in Española on horseback during Lent, and on the way home, between Abiquiu and Española, they spotted a strange looking object on the side of the road about a hundred yards away. As they approached it, it suddenly jumped out in the road in front of them. It was about two feet high and looked like a little ghost because it was completely white. They said it was a *monita,* a little white doll, wearing a white cloak. It had a scary looking face with big sad eyes. Its mouth was open, like it was screaming, but there was no sound. The horses tried to get around it, but the *monita* came toward them real fast and then it moved alongside the horses. The horses then bolted and started galloping down the road, but no matter how fast they ran, they couldn't shake the *monita.* It stayed next to them all the way to Abiquiu. My uncles were a mess by the time they got home. They both jumped off their horses and ran into the house and didn't look back. My grandmother looked out the window and said there was nothing there.

Other people saw the *monita* in the area during those times. They said it

La Llorona

was *La Llorona* punishing people for going to dances during Lent. I used to love hearing this story when I was growing up, even though it gave me the chills and bad dreams every time they told it to me.

Josie Martinez
Fairview, NM

The Owl at the Cemetery

In the early 1930s, when the penitentiary was located on Pen Road in Santa Fe, and the warden was a man named Swope, a lot of the local people had jobs there and they used to bring home some pretty interesting stories, as you can imagine.

My grandmother told us that one night, as one of the guards, a guy named Tafoya, was heading home in his car, an owl flew into the headlights and stayed in front of his car as he drove. He became mesmerized by this owl and started following it. He was powerless to do anything else and the car even seemed to drive itself. It led him to the graveyard off Cordova Road and Early Street – the Guadalupe Cemetery. He stopped his car when he got there and he just left the lights on, staring through the windshield and watching the owl. The owl was flying all over, in and out among the headstones. It disappeared behind one of them and then, all of a sudden, from behind this same headstone appeared a woman dressed all in black, crying and wailing. She came toward him, walking into the headlights while pointing back in the direction of the headstone and indicating that she wanted him to do something, but he couldn't figure out what it was.

He was so terrified that he just sat there, frozen, for what seemed to be an eternity. He eventually got his wits about him, put the car into reverse, backed up as fast he could, and sped home.

He went back to the cemetery the following day to see what headstone the woman had been pointing at, and he found that it was for an infant that had died at a very tender age – just a few months old. My grandmother told me it had been *La Llorona* in the cemetery that night, and that she was telling me this story because she didn't want me to go into that cemetery or any other cemetery, for that matter. She needn't have worried!

There's more to the story, though. *La Llorona* had quite a reputation in those days – people were always claiming to have seen her, especially after a few drinks at the local *cantina* – and this fellow Tafoya got very excited that he had actually met her face to face, that this was the real thing! The trouble is that no one believed him, not even his own wife or mother. And no matter how he tried to convince them, they just never quite bought the story, even when he took them to the cemetery and pointed out the grave of *La Llorona's* child.

It was said that this Tafoya used to wander the streets of the different *barrios* telling the story over and over. And of course, the more he told it, the less people believed. He left his job and began to spend more and more time at the Guadalupe Cemetery, apparently hoping to see *La Llorona* just once more.

He died at a young age, bewitched by the memory of *La Llorona.*

Yvonne C. Roybal
Los Angeles, CA

Postscript

On the night I finished proofreading the manuscript for this book, I had a very bizarre experience which I am sure is connected to *La Llorona*. Two days later, another strange thing occurred, and I believe very strongly that these events are interconnected. Both occurred at my house near Rodeo Road in Santa Fe, which I understand to be an area that had many *La Llorona* sightings before the developers started building houses there in the 1960s. Before then, Rodeo Road and the area around it was a desolate but beautiful area full of arroyos and *chamisa* bushes where people came to hunt rabbits, ride horses, and take walks.

The first incident occurred on a cold night in February, when I was telling my husband about some of the stories I had read that day. I was standing outside the bedroom in the doorway and my husband was lying on the bed. I had just turned my back and was walking away when I felt a presence behind me just inside the bedroom door. It was so strong that I jerked my head around to see who was there. Of course, there was no one, but I felt as though I could have reached out and easily touched whoever it was.

Two days later, I was alone in the house with my two sons, then four and six. We were all seated at the kitchen table, eating supper. Suddenly, Robert, the little one, turned and looked in the direction of the same place where I had felt the presence two days before. He jumped down from the chair and yelled "Daddy!" and ran toward something that only he could see, his arms outstretched in anticipation. Frightened, I also jumped up and ran after Robert and grabbed his shoulders. "What did you see?" I asked him.

For the next few minutes, Robert insisted that he had seen someone. Finally, he said, "Maybe it was a cat." When he understood that it could not have been a cat, he said, "I saw something there, and it was gray." He would not back down from his story. What he saw was as real to him as anything he had ever seen.

I sat the boys down at the table and forced myself to walk through the house. I checked the closets, under the beds, everywhere. The windows and doors were locked. We were alone in the house.

Someone told me later that *La Llorona* would sometimes appear to women with young children. Remembering that my neighbor also had two little boys, I mentioned it to her the next day and asked her if she had ever had a similar experience or had ever heard a woman weeping in the greenbelt area next to her house. She looked at me strangely and said, "How funny you should ask me that. Last weekend, I heard a terrible scream. At first I thought it was a cat, but it didn't really sound like a cat at all. My husband and I couldn't figure out what it was."

I believe that what my neighbor heard and what my son saw was *La Llorona*. So, a word to the wise: Do not read these stories with a skeptical heart, or you, too, may summon *La Llorona* to your home!

Lisa Sena
Santa Fe, NM

About the Author and Illustrator

Judith Shaw Beatty has lived in Santa Fe, New Mexico for forty-six years. She has been a contributing editor to HuffPost (where the account of her battle with a severe case of polio was widely circulated on social media) and is on the staff of US Represented, an e-magazine dedicated to free speech and creative expression. [Visit judithshawbeatty.com]

Anita Otilia Rodriguez grew up on Taos Plaza. As a painter, writer, historian, cook and activist, her paintings and her book, "Coyota in the Kitchen," reflect the culture, historical experience and mystery of her beloved New Mexico. [Visit www.anitarodriguez.com]

Made in the USA
Coppell, TX
22 December 2019